FALLING FOR CINDERELLA

PREETHI VENUGOPALA

Contents

Contents

Acknowledgements

Writing during a pandemic is difficult. But writing this story was what kept me away from worrying about what was happening in the outside world. In a way, this story kept me sane. The main issue was carving out time to sit down and write it. Maids were absent and I had extra chores added to my daily routine. I had to take on the role of teacher, cook, barber and cleaner. Thankfully, I still found time to write.

Thank you to all my writer friends who are the best cheerleaders ever.

As always, a BIG thank you to my dear husband Venugopala and my son Akshaj for being my cheerleaders. I love you both.

A big thank you to my editor Nikita who did a commendable job even while dealing with myriad problems.

Thank you, God, for helping me find happiness through writing.

Lastly, thank you, dear reader, for picking this book. You are my favourite person in the world.

Preethi Venugopala

What you seek,
is seeking you
-RUMI

1

CHANDNI

Every once in a while, when books transported me into unknown worlds, I gathered impossible dreams from them and weaved my own little fairy tales. Through them, I opened magical portals that led me into lands where life was a long, thrilling adventure. But in reality, my life was filled with nonstop misadventures that never seemed to end.

My current situation promised to be the perfect recipe for a disaster. I shouldn't have agreed to this. But was there even another option?

I winced as one of the hired beauticians worked on my untouched eyebrows. I had never felt the need to trim them. Two others were waxing my legs and arms, respectively.

"Hurry up! We don't have all the time in the world. The party begins at eight." Neeru Aunty snapped at the beauticians.

It was only six now. What was the hurry?

Once she completed shaping my eyebrows, the beautician set out to work on my hair, trimming them into layers and styling them. My hair felt soft like silk, courtesy of the multiple hair treatments I had sat through. I might have loved this experience if the very thought of what awaited me in the next few hours didn't make my knees go weak.

Whenever someone entered the room we were in, through the open door, I glimpsed servants hurrying past carrying flowers, fruit bowls and vessels, getting things ready for the party. Parties at Malhotra Mansion were not new to me. Never had I been a part of such celebrations, nor had I wished to be a part of them.

Ever since I remembered, Malhotra Mansion, situated in the city of dreams Mumbai, has been my home. When Grandmother was alive, the cosy little bedroom on the second floor had belonged to us. The day after she died, I had been asked to shift to a small bedroom in the annexe attic. My old bedroom had been converted to one of the four guest bedrooms in the mansion. That was three years ago.

According to Grandma, if God hadn't been so cruel, my life would have been different. I would have inherited the Malhotra Group—or the Venus Group as it had been once called. When my father had founded it twenty years ago, it had been a small-scale textile industry. Within ten years, he had turned it into a public limited company with profits increasing manifold every year. But tragedy struck in the twelfth year of its existence.

Ratan Malhotra, the son of Grandma's sister, had become the major shareholder of the Venus Group after the untimely death of my father. He renamed it overnight to give it a face-lift after the scandalous death of its founder.

Apparently, plagued by losses, father had taken the shortcut to escape from his troubles. I only have vague memories of that fateful day at the resort in Bali. But sometimes, I still woke up in the middle of the night, choked by tears and guilt weighing like lead inside my chest. Survivor's guilt. I should have died along with my parents. Hadn't they planned just that?

"I owe a lot to Ram *bhaiyya.* You will continue to stay with us. I will take care of you from now on." That was what Ratan Uncle had told me on the day Grandma passed away.

Of course, he took care of me. I was packed off to the annexe the same day. From then on, the Malhotras, who were renowned Scrooges, forced me to earn my keep. Once I returned from college, I became their all-around help. I had to step in for whatever was the pressing job at the time. These days, I was a part-time gardener one day; on another day, I was doing chores in the kitchen and on yet another, I would be housekeeping. I ate food with the other staff and hardly found time to study.

When Grandma was alive, after she fought yet another time with Neeru Aunty, she would curse me and blame me for my parents' death.

"You are an unlucky girl, Chandni. Else, why would my son kill himself? Ever since you were born, his business started to fail. You shouldn't have wandered out that day; you should have died with them."

The very next minute she would apologise and cry.

"Devil take my tongue. That wretched Neeru gets on my nerves every single time. If my Ram had been alive, he would have raised you like a princess," she would say as she wiped her own and my tears.

I had grown up wearing hand-me-down clothes of Lavanya, the only daughter of the Malhotras, and cherished playing with her discarded toys. We were good friends in childhood and had remained so until money induced disparities started corrupting the bond we shared. The glue that bonded us was Grandma. But the bond started to weaken due to the quarrels between Neeru Aunty and Grandma.

Grandma's fights with Neeru Aunty were always on the same topic. According to Grandma, the Malhotras were living off the efforts of her son. In retaliation for this accusation, Neeru Aunty treated Grandma like trash. She never missed a chance to humiliate her in front of her guests, after insisting on Grandma's presence at her kitty parties. Neeru Aunty loved boasting about how she and her husband were taking care of Ram Khanna's old mother and daughter. After each fight, their hostility increased. I often begged Grandma to not attend them. Grandma, however, found peace if she could hurl a few insults back at Neeru Aunty whenever she got an opportunity. She loved keeping scores.

Caught in between, I found solace in my books and studies.

"You got your father's brains, child! Didn't he singlehandedly build the Malhotra empire? You make me proud." Grandma had hugged me tight when I got the 9th rank in the 12th board exams. My rank had helped me land a seat in my dream college in Mumbai. That too with a scholarship provided by a charity foundation that had tied up with the school I attended.

Neeru Aunty hated that I had gained admission into the same college as her daughter. Grandma had passed away during my final semester in college leaving me completely at the mercy of the Malhotras.

Luckily, Ratan Uncle had stepped in when I graduated with a high rank and granted me one of the educational scholarships given by the Malhotra Group for talented students. The scholarship helped me enrol for an MBA course in the same college. But after class, Neeru Aunty made sure I helped in the kitchen, ran errands and cleaned bathrooms and toilets while Lavanya, who was my classmate, roamed around the town partying. By the time the day ended, I would have energy only to crash into bed.

Somehow, I managed to do all the college work early in the morning and studied during lunch hours. My friends, Vani and Shweta, who knew my predicament helped me with assignments and exams whenever possible.

College would have been fun if Lavanya wasn't a bitch of the highest order. Taking a cue from her mother, nowadays, she didn't lose a chance to insult me in front of our classmates. She would hurl snide comments at me randomly and she would often make me carry her things. If somebody questioned her, she would say, "Oh she is used to that. After all, she is our servant."

It didn't help that the Malhotras, who used to be filthy rich, were now going through a very bleak period financially. But they always tried to prove to the outside world that all was well. Neeru Aunty had by now relinquished all hopes that her ageing husband would revive their slowly dying business. She had pinned all her hope on Lavanya.

"She has to marry into a rich household. That's the only way." That had become her mantra nowadays.

Lavanya was beautiful and would certainly snag a rich man as a husband. She had the looks and with a mother like hers, who paraded her like some hallowed jewel, she was not far from landing herself a prized groom. But it was an almost open secret that she was a drug addict. Last night, she had gone out with her friends and had to be hospitalized after a drug overdose.

The media had got the scent of the news and had hounded the Malhotras for an update.

"What rubbish! Lavanya is fine. I don't know where you guys get your info from. She will be the hostess for her birthday party happening at home tonight. We will be sending pictures to the media and posting them on our social media handles as well." Ratan Uncle had declared to the media right from the courtyard of the Malhotra Mansion today morning as I was leaving for college.

When I arrived at the mansion after college, Neeru Aunty had simply told me what had to be done.

"You will take Lavanya's place at today's party. She will be at the recovery centre this whole week. Be ready to pay back all the kindness we have showered on you."

Kindness? They made me work like a mule and never said a word of appreciation. My chores were increasing every day because Neeru Aunty was being forced to tighten her purse strings.

Lavanya and I were of similar colouring, age and build. That was what made Neeru aunty come up with this elaborate ruse to ward off all the bad press her daughter had attracted. Their future depended upon it. I was a nobody; nobody knew me socially. Also, I knew practically everything about Lavanya. As we studied for the same course, I could handle conversations in that area too.

I still couldn't understand what they were going to do with my face and my overall look. Lavanya had inherited her mother's round face and did not resemble me at all. Also, she looked like she had stepped out of the pages of a fashion magazine, with her flawless skin and attire to match. She always dressed in designer clothes. I had never seen the insides of a beauty salon nor had I ever worn anything other than casual clothes.

"It's going to be a masquerade. A masked party. The theme we've selected is fairy tales. You'll be dressed up as Cinderella and wearing a mask that will cover most of your face," Neeru Aunty had said when I'd voiced my doubt.

Very well, I'd thought. I could play the role of Cinderella. The fairy tale that I could relate the most to was that of Cinderella. I lived in an attic and worked as a maid at the Malhotra Mansion. I could play Cinderella perfectly if all I had to do was, mop, sweep and clean. But here, I was being asked to perform in the second half of the story where Cinderella goes to the ball and meets the prince. Just the thought terrified me.

"I will be around to rescue you if you make a blunder. If you do it right, you can take a whole week off from work," said Neeru Aunty, patting my shoulder. Then she looked upwards and prayed aloud, "Please *Bappa*, don't put any hurdles in the paths of my daughter. Let tonight pass as smoothly as I've envisioned. I'll fast for a full day in your honour then."

I quickly turned away to hide my smile. Neeru Aunty couldn't go without eating for even an hour. Fasting for a full day was indeed the biggest sacrifice she could make.

"Go, take a quick bath and come. Don't wash your hair. We need to get you dressed and ready in another hour," said the main beautician.

The hours-long torture had finally ended. I sighed in relief. I wondered why Lavanya and the other girls in my class did this religiously every month. Picking up my glasses from the table, I perched them on my nose and glanced into the mirror. My jaws dropped. Gone was the country bumpkin who was ridiculed for her oily hair and bushy eyebrows. Add a bit of makeup, the mask and the costume, I might pass off easily as Lavanya. I took off my glasses and glanced into the mirror without them.

The main beautician smiled kindly at me and spoke, "You are lovely. You should groom yourself more often."

Muttering thanks, I turned away and walked into the hall of the mansion only to encounter a furry ball that leapt onto my legs. Bruno! The only member of the Malhotra family who loved me to bits. Crouching down, I scratched the ears of the cute pug. He licked my face, making me giggle.

"Yes, I love you too. Now let me go and get ready. Else, Aunty will box my ears," I whispered to Bruno. Bruno got down from my lap and sat on his rug, making his usual sad face. I dropped a kiss on his forehead and walked towards the annexe. I often felt as though he understood me completely. Some evenings, once I was done with my chores, I would sit on the bench in the backyard of the house and talk to him. He would make appropriate noises wherever needed and I'd feel as if I had spoken to a friend.

After taking a bath, I applied a homemade cream all over my body. Grandma had taught me how to make it using the *parijat* blossoms that bloomed in the courtyard of the local Krishna temple. I often made portions of the cream for Vani and Shweta, who loved the scent and the effectiveness of the cream.

"Patent this. You should start a cosmetics firm in the future. My younger sister steals it from me all the time. I swear it will make you a millionaire one day. This is one amazing cream," Vani often said.

It sounded like dialogue from a movie. Almost everyone among the staff used the flower for various things. It was considered holy and my grandmother always thanked the flowers and prayed before making the cream or the flower oil. I followed all her rituals religiously.

By the time I returned to the mansion, the dress I was to wear and the shoes for the occasion had arrived after an alteration. Lavanya was a size bigger than me and my feet were a size smaller than Lavanya's. Last-minute changes had created chaos but the designers were seasoned professionals and had sent what we needed on time.

The dress won over my heart immediately. It was an off-shoulder lavender tulle gown with a sweetheart neckline. Ruffles made of soft lavender fur cascaded down the front making the dress very fairytale-like. It was nothing like any dress I had ever worn. It would take a little while for me to get used to the grandeur. The transparent pumps were yet another marvel. Soft and very comfortable. I couldn't believe that I would be wearing these in a while.

Once the beauticians had done my hair and makeup, they helped me wear the gown. I felt like a princess. I had never considered myself a beauty. I couldn't help but admit though that I now looked lovely. A little bit of grooming and makeup had indeed made an ordinary girl like me look like an heiress.

When I picked up my glasses to wear them, the beauticians stopped me.

"You can see without those glasses, right? We cannot let you wear them today. Lavanya doesn't wear glasses."

It would be okay. I had only a slight short-sightedness. I could easily manage without it. I turned when I heard a gasp from behind me. It was Neeru Aunty.

"You clean up well. It is a pity that no one will know it is you. You will be wearing this after all," said Neeru Aunty, entering the room brandishing a shiny mask. Her eyes twinkled with malice. She was dressed in a red designer gown, the cost of which would have been sufficient to fund my entire college education. But on her, it looked shapeless and unappealing. She almost looked like a luxury pillow.

Neeru Aunty handed over the shiny purple mask to me. My heart sank as I wore the mask. It covered most of my face.

Pity. Nobody would recognize me. Just like Neeru Aunty said and wanted.

When they all left me alone, I took off the mask and clicked pictures of myself in the gown on my phone. I also made one of the beauticians click a full-length picture. The fifth-generation iPhone was a hand-me-down from Neeru aunty, who now owned the latest one. I had rejoiced when she had given it to me one day.

"Use it. I don't want you to be late for work. It will also help when I need you to pick up laundry or do any other chore."

I looked fondly at the pictures on the phone. I also took a pic after wearing the mask. Cinderella was ready for a magical night. Only, in my case, I would not be meeting a prince tonight. But billionaires. At least half a dozen of them.

The Malhotras invited only eligible, rich bachelors to their parties. The females at the party would be mostly married, engaged or over the age of fifty so that there wouldn't be a competition for their daughter. Inevitably, the bachelors would end up seeking out the belle of the ball.

"Come here, girl. Read through this list. These are the names of the bachelors who have been invited today. Lavanya knows all of them. Study them," said Neeru Aunty putting a stack of papers in front of me.

I read through the list. Except for one, none of the profiles impressed me. All born with a silver spoon in their mouth and living a life of splendour thanks to the money their ancestors had made. Though he fell into the same category, Karan Varma found a special place in my heart.

He was a billionaire in his own right and had conquered the world with his unique and innovative electronic gadgets. The majority of them were his inventions. He held more than 50 patents in his name.

I looked forward to meeting him and him alone, also because he was the reason I was still alive.

KARAN

My driver Raju was a pro at navigating the crowded lanes of Mumbai. Traffic today was moving slower than usual as it was the weekend. I returned my attention to my iPad and checked the box against the last item on my to-do list for the day.

Tame Desai.

If I had not wanted to meet Desai, who cancelled our meetings citing the vaguest of reasons, I would not have said yes to Malhotra's party invitation. It was typically one of those parties that were a vanity fair and *adda* for gold diggers. Srijan, my manager, had dug out inside information that Desai Jr, who was hunting for a bride, was attending the do. Though Desai Sr was giving me the slip, maybe I could convince the junior to become our supplier of organic herbs and vegetables. Anything organic was in great demand among the health-conscious upper class of Mumbai. Our food processing branch would greatly benefit if they signed an exclusive contract with us.

The four-storied Malhotra Mansion was shining like a bright jewel amidst the other apartments and villas in the street we had just entered. They seemed to have gone all out with the decorations. I had never attended their parties, although I had met the Malhotras many times socially and knew they were among the nouveau rich. Mom disliked Neeru Malhotra and would perhaps go berserk if she knew I was attending a party thrown by 'that obnoxious woman'. If the rumour mills were to be believed, they were on the verge of bankruptcy. Perhaps this was the final flare before their fire died forever.

Ratan Malhotra, the current chairman of Malhotra Group, stood at the entrance of the villa. He seemed delighted to see me. The plump man was dressed in a light blue suit that starkly clashed with his yellow sneakers.

"Welcome, welcome," shouted Mr Malhotra as he received me with a huge smile on his face. "Allow me to introduce my wife, Neeru."

Neeru Malhotra came forward to greet me with a huge grin on her face. Her heavily pencilled eyebrows, beady eyes and dark red lipstick reminded me of sleazy B-grade movie vamps. "Go on in, Karan. We will see to it that you have a good time. Would you like to wear a mask?"

After refusing to take the ornate mask she had offered, I scoured the crowd inside the courtyard for the presence of Desai Jr. Most men weren't wearing masks. But most women were. To my disappointment, I couldn't spot Desai Jr. among the people there. Maybe he had headed to the refreshment area. Had he started binging on alcohol so early? That was a slightly distressing thought. I needed him with a clear head until I convinced him.

"Karan, how nice of you to come to our bash. I think you haven't met our Lavanya yet," said Neeru Malhotra, as she hollered at her daughter. "Lavanya...come here."

"No, I haven't," I said, and pivoted on my heel to head to the bar area to avoid meeting the girl of whom I had heard nothing good when my gaze fell on the most exquisite girl I had ever seen. And I forgot to breathe.

Miss Lavanya Malhotra was breathtakingly beautiful. I couldn't see her features completely but she was even more gorgeous in real than in the photos. Her hair, shining like the softest silk, was pinned on her crown in a loose up-do exposing a creamy white neck and shapely shoulders that mesmerized me. Carefully ironed curls let down from the up-do tantalizingly fluttered near her cheeks in the light breeze. Her mask had hidden most of her face, but those lips alone were enough to tempt any warm-blooded man. Her smile and the graceful way in which she was walking toward me made me forget where I was and who she was. In my eyes, she had become the brightest star in the night sky, my guiding light.

She greeted me with a *namaste* and a shy smile. Not something I would have expected from an heiress. Inevitably, that simple gesture endeared her to me even more. I conveyed my birthday wishes and gave the bouquet Raju had picked up for me. I felt ashamed as the small bunch of flowers suddenly felt inadequate. This girl deserved something extraordinary. But somehow, in her hands, even that tiny bouquet looked lovely.

"Lavanya dear, why don't you show our guest around and make sure he is comfortable?" said Neeru Malhotra.

I could have kissed Mrs Malhotra for saying that. Desai Jr was soon forgotten. I followed like a happy puppy as Lavanya led me into the main hall where the party was raging. Pink and white floral decorations were everywhere. Just as we entered, music began to play and the men around started leading their partners to the dance floor.

"Shall we dance?" I asked, with my heart in my mouth.

"I don't know how to dance," she blurted out. Her soft voice added another layer of enchantment to her charm.

"Are you kidding me?" I asked as a slow romantic song began.

"No. I swear. I haven't ever danced. At least not at a party like this."

"Aha! That is okay. Where have you danced then?"

"Last time I danced, I was in the ninth grade. And I was dressed as a male," she said and let out a nervous giggle.

"That is enough. Come, let's dance," I said and extended my hand toward her.

"I don't know this kind of dance. I might step on your toes."

"There is only one rule for this dance. To sway with the music and have fun."

All the couples around us were waltzing. Lavanya had still not accepted my hand. She seemed to be looking at her mother for approval. She kept her palm on mine only after Neeru Malhotra nodded. Interesting.

How could the paparazzi paint such horrid pictures of this girl? Hadn't they said she lived to party and had a drug habit she couldn't seem to quit? They couldn't be talking about the timid girl in front of me. I wound my arm around her waist and pulled her toward me as we took our position among the crowd of slowly swaying couples. She gasped lightly. Softly, I guided her to place one hand on my shoulder and took her other hand in mine.

As if proving her former statement true, she stepped on my toes after a minute into the dance but quickly apologised.

"Never mind. I think you really need some private lessons before we dance again," I said with a snigger after she stepped on my foot yet another time.

"I told you! I am so sorry. Did it hurt?"

"I am glad you aren't wearing stilettos. I need my feet intact as I will be leaving for Amsterdam tomorrow evening."

"Oh, Amasterdam? Any plans to visit the tulips gardens? I guess it is too early for that? The tulips' season begins only in March, right?"

"It is a boring business trip. I haven't visited the tulip gardens until now. I never get the time to go sightseeing."

"That is a shame. I love tulips. A visit to Amsterdam during the tulip season is been on my bucket list since childhood."

"Why haven't you visited it then?"

Lavanya didn't answer for a long minute.

"Can you please stop asking questions? I am trying hard not to step on your foot again," she said, biting her lower lip.

I smiled. As far as I knew, the Malhotras travelled a lot. It was hard to believe that she hadn't visited Amsterdam yet. She had cleverly avoided answering my question.

The music ended then and I decided to leave the dance floor, much to the relief of my partner. Lavanya was surprising me with every minute I spent in her company. The urge to know more about her made me say something I never would have otherwise said.

"Can we take a stroll in your garden? The night is lovely and it will be a pity if I have to part company with you now."

Lavanya seemed a little surprised by my request. Again, she looked around as if searching for her mother. Neeru Malhotra was not anywhere around. Reluctantly, Lavanya guided me towards the door that opened into the garden. The landscaping was done tastefully and several flowers bloomed in the garden. The trimmed shrubs and the small decorative pool in the corner were all done aesthetically. The nip in the air and the fragrance of the blossoms along with the presence of the beauty beside me made my heart grow fonder.

"So, Lavanya, you are an MBA student, right?" I asked, wanting to make her talk as we strolled along the garden path.

"Yes. Second-year at St. Xaviers."

"Why management?"

"I guess the dynamics of money fascinate me. I am specialising in finance," she said.

"Interesting point of view. Do you know who I am, Lavanya?" I asked, hoping for the first time that my fame had preceded me.

"Yes, of course. Almost all the girls in my class are your fans."

"I wonder why!" I exclaimed though I was aware of the kind of fan following I had among the youngsters. The last time I had gone to visit a cousin at her hostel, I had been surrounded by a band of enthusiastic girls who had done everything possible to garner my attention.

"Are you fishing for compliments, Mr Varma? The Financial Chronicle listed you as the hottest bachelor in India. And you won a world business award just last week," she concluded with a smile on her face as if her explanation justified the crazy behaviour of the girls.

"I don't care what they think about me. I would like to know the opinion of this girl though," I said, my gaze returning fondly to her lovely features as we paused in the path.

Just then, a soft bark sounded from near and what seemed like a ball of fur dashed toward us. A little pug came to a stop in front of me and continued to bark furiously.

"Ah, my hero, Bruno! Came to my rescue, huh?"

Lavanya squatted near the pet and started to give him a tummy rub. The pug eyed me suspiciously even as he purred in satisfaction.

A servant, who was perhaps in charge of the pug, came out, apologised to both of us and led the pug inside.

"Such a cute rescuer. But you need not worry. I don't have any evil intentions," I said. We can usually judge a person by the way they treat their pets. This girl was surprising me at every turn. I had every intention to know more about her before the night ended.

"I am not scared of you. You don't seem like someone who would take advantage of a girl," said Lavanya.

The way she said that stirred something inside me. Did anyone try to take advantage of her? My blood boiled at the very thought. I couldn't understand this wild urge I felt to protect this girl, cherish her and keep her happy.

If I were to believe the gossip magazines, Lavanya had had a string of affairs. I had believed it seeing her pictures. She was a stunner. Now, up close, she was angelic. But those appalling titbits of gossip seemed entirely false. This girl in front of me looked guileless. I would wager my whole life that she hadn't even been kissed before. And suddenly, I wanted to be the one to initiate her into the world of love, of sensual touches and feelings.

Had any girl ever made me feel this way? The mad urge to tug her close was strong. So strong, that resisting it was beginning to frustrate me. I might scare her if I did that. I didn't want that.

So, we rambled along the garden path silently, listening to the strains of music emanating from the house. Even that stroll felt enchanting. And suddenly, she stopped. *'Main agar kahoon tumsa hasin...'* from the Bollywood movie *Om Shanti Om* was playing from the speakers.

"I love this song. It is my all-time favourite. We should have been dancing to this song. Then I wouldn't have stepped on your toes perhaps. It is that groovy," she said, turning around to face me.

"Let's dance here then," I said impulsively. Without waiting for her reply, I wound my arms around her waist and pulled her closer. I liked how she didn't resist. I liked how she placed her palms on my chest.

"But the music is not that clear. Maybe we should go back," she said softly.

"Listen harder," I whispered, moving my lips closer to her left ear. Her proximity was making my heart go wild. "*Main agar kahoon tumsa haseen, kaynaat mein nahi hai kahin, tareef yeh bhi to sach hai kuch bhi nahi,*" I sang to her in sync with the song flowing out from the speakers.

"Wow, you sing so well," she said in a voice filled with awe and looked up into my eyes. Our eyes met, duelled and I held them captive. Never had I been proud of my singing than at that moment. There was magic in the air, certainly.

Suddenly every word of the song I was singing sounded like the truth. My truth. She was indeed the prettiest being in the universe. Nothing else was true. I meant every word I sang. I was falling. Falling rapidly in love with the Cinderella in my arms.

3

CHANDNI

This was beyond any of my wildest dreams. I was dancing in the arms of Karan. He was without doubt the most handsome man I had ever seen. He looked more attractive now than when I had met him briefly during graduation. Even the stars of Bollywood paled in front of him. That day he had held my hand and walked me back to life. Today, he was perhaps going to give me a heart attack.

The day Karan Varma had come to our college to give a talk on 'Advances in Technology' had been one of the lowest periods in my life. Grandmother had passed away unexpectedly the previous month. Life had never been as difficult for me as it was then. Lavanya was acting the craziest, Neeru aunty had asked me to start working as their maid to pay my keep and I was trailing on the studies front due to how hectic life had suddenly become.

The terrace above the indoor auditorium was one of my favourite spots on the campus. Not only did it give a birds-eye view of the entire city, but it was also one of the very few spots on the campus that were mostly devoid of troublemakers or couples owing to its proximity to the college admin office.

On that gloomy Thursday, I had gone to my chosen spot of tranquillity to get over the barrage of insults and temper tantrums thrown by Lavanya. Leaning against the parapet wall, I stood on the ledge and gazed at the city of Mumbai stretched far in front of me. I was filled with melancholy as thoughts about Grandma came calling. In the vastness of this world, I had no one to call my own, not even a single soul. As tears rushed down from my eyes, I began to question my very existence. I had failed the only human being who had been dependent on me. I hadn't been near her when she needed me the most. Perilous thoughts had begun to flit around in my mind.

Why was I even alive?

For what?

Was there anything left for me in this world?

Shouldn't it be easy to just end it all right now?

I'd leaned forward and looked down at the ground below. It could all end so fast.

"Don't even think about it!" A voice floated toward me and a strong hand pulled me away from the ledge.

It had been Karan Varma. Apparently, he had decided to take a breath of fresh air on the terrace before he gave his speech. My tear smeared face must have convinced him that I was about to jump off. I didn't even have the energy to deny it. He sat me down on one of the cement benches on the terrace and talked to me.

It had been easy to talk to him, a total stranger. I told him how Grandma had died, how she had lain on the cold floor waiting for help to arrive. How I had become an orphan.

Towards the end, when I had burst out sobbing, he had squeezed my hand and said, "We all die eventually. That is the only truth in this world. But when we are traversing the path of life, we should strive to live. It is a man who is outwardly courageous that dares to die. A man who is courageous from within dares to live. I have been where you are now and can empathize with you completely. Face your problems head-on and do not run away from them. Trust me, it gets better even before you realise."

His manager had arrived then to remind him that it was time for him to get on stage. Patting my shoulders, Karan had said, "Sit in the front row today so that I can see you while I speak. Can you do that?"

I nodded. He had been perhaps worried that I might jump the moment he turned his back.

As he talked about how technology was improving human life, his words about life and the need to survive were buzzing in my mind. As if I had been in his thoughts even then, he talked about apps that helped to meditate, rant, to contact doctors, counsellors, and many other miracles offered by technology. By the time he finished his talk, I had decided never to lose trust in life again. Whatever it took, I was going to become a survivor. I had hit rock bottom already; the only path left to take was to crawl the way back up.

Before he left the campus, Karan had slipped his business card into my hand.

"Call or email whenever you feel low. You have a friend in me, got it?" he had said with a smile that had touched the very core of my heart.

That had been two and a half years ago. I'd never called or mailed him. I knew it was a gesture of kindness on his part but I hadn't wanted to bother him anymore. I didn't want him to remember me as someone who had given up on life. I wanted him to see me as a person filled with light. Not someone drowning in darkness. And that was what I had set out to be from then on. I had decided to become my own superhero, my own saviour.

Now, years later, I was dancing in his arms. Not because I believed I had become worthy of his affections, but because of a charade initiated by my scheming aunt. A part of me wanted to tell him that I was not Lavanya. But the other part selfishly wanted me to be Lavanya, for whom this could be her everyday reality. I could then dream of being his lover, and talk about things I loved with him every single day for the rest of my life.

Karan was asking questions and I continued answering them. It was only when I had told him about my likes and dislikes that I realized that I had forgotten to play the role of Lavanya. I had told him exactly what I liked. Not what Lavanya liked. I let out a defeated sigh.

"Am I tiring you out already?" asked Karan. The twinkle in his eyes made me feel guilty. How could I forget that this was just a charade? It would end exactly at midnight when the party ended.

But I didn't want it to end. I wanted to make this night memorable for Karan. For the kindness he had showered on me when I had needed it the most.

I wanted to gift this reckless night to myself as well. I wanted to feel cherished the way Karan was making me feel. I wanted to twirl and dance in his arms the whole night.

As we continued to dance listening to the music that floated towards us, Karan's arms tightened around my waist and pulled me closer.

"So, tell me Lavanya, why do I feel like you are unhappy? As if you dread being in my presence?"

"No... Nothing of the sort. You are imagining things."

I was scared, alright. I feared that I might spill my secret. I didn't want to lie to him. I was being dragged into something like a trance via his words and his actions. I was worried I might tear off the mask, confess that I was not Lavanya and surrender to his charms. He should not be deceived in any way. All I wanted was his happiness.

And then, to my horror, I found myself staring at his lips. I couldn't look away. I wanted to be kissed, to be loved by Karan. The urge was getting stronger every other second. Was the same thought hovering in Karan's mind as well? His eyes seemed focused on my lips the next time I checked. A blush crept up my cheeks and my lips curved up in a smile.

"You look so lovely when you smile. Tell me, what were you thinking about just now?"

I was taken aback by his direct question. There was no way I could tell him the truth.

"I cannot possibly tell you that. What do you think I was thinking about?" I countered.

"If your thoughts were wandering along the same lanes as my own, they would be pretty scandalous," said Karan with a mischievous sparkle in his eyes.

I wanted to know exactly what he was thinking about. I could guess though as his gaze landed on my lips again. I would have felt violated if anyone else had done the same. But when Karan's gaze fell on my lips, they bloomed. I wanted to tilt my chin up and offer my lips to him, to be kissed. Thoroughly. It was madness and I knew it. Yet I did exactly that.

I lifted my chin slightly and looked straight into Karan's eyes. Did the yearning inside me reflect in my eyes? Perhaps it did, because the next moment, Karan had moved closer and cupped my face. Then, very slowly, he pressed his lips to mine. Just a feather touch. My heart thudded. Karan paused and looked into my eyes as if to ensure I was not offended. I heard him groan as he claimed my lips again. This time with a passion that made me forget who I was. I felt like a princess. If Cinderella had lived all those years ago, perhaps this was how she might have felt when the prince kissed her.

"God, what are you doing to me, love?" Karan whispered as he held me tight. "You smell like *parijats*. It is delicious. And I am in love with this tiny little mole," he said pressing his lips on the tiny black mole on my shoulder, just below my left ear. Every inch of skin that his lips touched, came alive.

When his warm lips roamed recklessly downward from my throat, I shuddered. I should have pushed him off. This would have been acceptable behaviour if we had been lovers. But we were nothing of the sort. We had met just an hour ago. Any moment now, Neeru Aunty would come and order me to return to the party. Yet, I couldn't stop him. I wanted him to kiss my aching bosom that I had never thought to be this sensitive. I liked what his lips were doing to my body. Heat began pooling in my belly as he continued worshipping me with his lips. My knees felt like jelly and I held onto him desperately. What was happening to me?

As if he knew this was wrong, Karan lifted his face from my bosom.

"I can't seem to stop. You are making me behave like a lunatic. Make it stop, love." Karan's voice sounded troubled.

Love! He had called me 'love'. This was not good. I was about to step away when Karan stopped me by holding onto my hand.

"Not so soon. I am not ready to part with you. Not yet, Lavanya," said Karan.

Lavanya. How had I forgotten? Karan's passion was directed at Lavanya, the Malhotra heiress. Not at Chandni, the poor relation of the Malhotras.

"I am sorry. But I must go. If anyone saw me alone with you like this, it would become a scandal," I said as I struggled to make him let me go.

"You are not a stranger to scandals, are you? Your father knows exactly how to handle scandals."

"I know. But I don't want to create one for you. You do not deserve to be dragged into meaningless scandals."

"What if I wished to be dragged into one with you? Better, let's create a scene that the press would remember," said Karan.

He must have been joking. Who wanted to attract scandals one after the other? Being with Lavanya meant just that. I should offend him and make him regret that he had tried to befriend a girl like Lavanya. Lavanya didn't deserve him. He seemed like a nice person. He didn't deserve a disaster like Lavanya.

My muddled thoughts must have become visible on my face because Karan chuckled and gently squeezed my hands before pulling me towards him.

"You take my breath away. See what you do to me," he said softly as he placed my right hand on his heart. I could feel it thudding through the layers of his clothing. Mesmerized by its rhythm, I gazed at him. The intensity of his dark eyes entrapped me. My own heart thudded as if to match his beat. But this was wrong. I shouldn't trap Karan. He deserved someone better.

"Karan, we need to go back inside. I am feeling cold. Neeru... I mean Mom would be furious if she found me alone with you here."

"Sorry, I have been so thoughtless," said Karan. He shrugged out of his dinner jacket and wrapped it around me. His scent, his warmth enveloped me. I trembled as he continued in a low but steady voice, "I want her to find us together. Then maybe I can take matters a bit further. I want to know you better, Lavanya. Something more should come out of this chance encounter. I find you intriguing."

"I am just an ordinary girl. Maybe this whole dreamlike facade, this mask, is adding to the mystery," I muttered.

"Exactly. I want it to end. I want to see your full face," said he, and before I could stop him, deftly removed my mask.

My jaw dropped as Karan's gaze landed on my face. With a gasp, I turned away.

"You are not Lavanya. Who are you?" cried Karan, holding my arms and making me face him. His eyes searched my face.

"I am sorry. I cannot answer that. You shouldn't have removed the mask," I said. I freed myself from his arms, pivoted on my heels and dashed away.

I ran without looking back. Karan would be hating me. I had lied and acted in the most disreputable manner. I had behaved freely with a stranger. I had even allowed him to kiss me. But strangely, I didn't regret any of it. I would treasure the moments I spent in his arms.

I ran straight into Neeru Aunty whose face was now almost the same colour as her gown. She stared at Karan and then at me.

I shuddered. I had failed to follow her instructions. I had exposed my face before Karan. If some photographer had spotted me without the mask, that would have become the next worst scandal for the Malhotras.

"Ungrateful girl! Leave before any reporter finds you. Take the back door."

My dreamy night out as Cinderella had ended. As I rushed through the back door to the annexe, I heard the clock in the main hall chime twelve times. I indeed felt like

Cinderella running from the ball. Instead of leaving behind a glass slipper, I was leaving with the jacket of my prince.

The prince would never come in search of me, he already seemed appalled by my deception. Given the way Neeru Aunty had glared at me, she would make sure that every single one of my dreams ended up as a heap of ashes.

As I wiped the tears away, I prayed fervently that Karan did not hate me for what I had done. I hoped he did not brand me as a liar.

I removed Karan's jacket and hugged it to my heart as tears began to flow. And then, as I breathed in his scent, hope dared to raise its fair head again.

KARAN

My first urge was to follow her and stop her. She was not Lavanya. That much I was sure of. Who was she?

Was I offended or relieved by the fact that she had lied to me? Even while we were talking, I'd been troubled by the vast difference between the reality that I perceived and the rumours I had heard.

Lavanya had always been painted by the press as an arrogant heiress who was borderline neurotic.

The girl who had been with me for the last two hours had been coy, down to earth and very much lovable. Who was she? Was she an actress paid to step in for Lavanya? As rumoured, Lavanya must be still in the hospital.

Strangely, I felt bereft and didn't have the wish to stay another minute at the party. The girl who had charmed me had surely gone. Though my heart ordered me to go in search of her, I didn't listen to it. She had been playing a role and had almost fooled me into believing that she was Lavanya.

One thing was crystal clear to me. The Malhotras had put her up to the task. And like a fool, I had fallen into their trap. I had initially thought of her as someone with a pure heart. Now I wasn't sure at all. All the questions raised by my brain now made absolute sense.

Why then did I feel a sense of loss as soon as I left the party? A part of me still wanted to go back in and search for the mystery girl. That was not prudent. I couldn't afford to fall victim to the schemes of such people. I had other important things to do. Nonetheless, the last two hours had been pleasant and memorable.

It was when I sat in my car that I realized that she'd taken my jacket with her. That too when Raju asked me about it. When had I become so absent-minded? I wasn't exactly sure what this meant or even if it indeed meant something.

It wasn't likely that I would see her again. My stubborn heart protested that this was not the last time. If it had been a one-time thing, I wouldn't have felt this much attachment. We had connected at some deeper level. No, it wasn't physical attraction alone. That had been there, no doubt, like a raging fire that would have consumed me wholly, if it had not been appeased by those kisses and caresses.

At some moment during our time together, perhaps our souls had touched one another. There was something intense about the way I felt about her. My thoughts were revolving non-stop around an unnamed entity.

I didn't believe in destiny. I had never been tempted to believe in it either. Nor had I ever listened to my heart. I ruthlessly went after the things I wished for and made them mine. But this, I would leave to fate. If this mystery girl was in my destiny, our paths would cross again. And strangely, I wanted that to happen. Except, I wasn't ready to do anything to that effect.

As my car meandered through the busy lanes, I relived the moments when my Cinderella had been in my arms. Her fragrance was unique; her satiny, soft skin had dazzled me. I would never forget the stunning face the mask had hidden behind it. If I were to meet her again, I'd recognise her in any crowd. Even if I didn't, I would compare every face I beheld to hers and find it lacking. She had forever jinxed me with her charm. Those tempting lips, those doe-like eyes and that sculpted face; the taste of her lips still lingered on my own.

If this wasn't love, I knew not what it was.

Yet, as time ticked past, I decided to let it all rest for a while. As of now, my thoughts had become unusually muddled. I would sleep on this and decide what to do in the morning. Yes, that was the best strategy.

When I reached home, our housekeeper, Anthony, let me in with his usual 'Welcome back, Sir!'. I nodded in acknowledgement.

"Is Mom sleeping?"

"Yes, she went to bed directly after dinner, complaining of a headache."

His answer sent a shiver of dread through me. Pausing, I turned to face Anthony. Was it anything serious?

"Everything alright? Book an appointment with the doctor if it hasn't gone by morning."

"She said it's nothing to worry about. She had forgotten to wear her glasses when she went out this afternoon. The headache is because of that."

Relief flooded me. Years ago, his careless attitude towards his health had claimed the life of my father. I still remembered how jovially Dad had gone to bed that day after spending a happy hour talking with me and mom. He had not woken up the next day. I had cursed myself for the longest time for not realizing that he was ill. Ever since then, whenever Mom fell ill, I panicked. I made a mental note to check on Mom first thing in the morning.

I had a very disturbed sleep that night. The masked beauty from the party appeared in every single one of my dreams.

What was this madness?

How could I get rid of it?

To clear my thoughts, I went out for a run early the next morning. Memories of her voice, her smile and her laughter kept me company even then. I pushed myself to exhaustion trying to get rid of them. By the time I returned, I was worn out mentally and physically. To my disappointment, my idiotic heart was still stuck in the time when she had been near me.

Every thought revolved around her. Was there a way to stop this?

A cold shower later, I felt a lot calmer and joined mom for breakfast. She was beaming rather unusually when I placed a kiss on her cheeks.

"Congratulations! You made headlines again," said Mom, as she pushed the day's newspaper towards me.

Goosebumps sprang up all over me as I noticed the photo in the article she was talking about. I grabbed the newspaper to take a closer look at the photo. We looked lovely together, my mystery princess and me. I was gazing at her like a besotted lover. I had indeed felt like one then. Even now, the magic had not truly worn off. The caption made me smile ruefully. The Malhotras had pulled it off.

"Business tycoon Karan dancing with the heiress of the Malhotra group. Romance in the air?"

I looked up when I heard Mom clearing her throat.

"I think I can die peacefully now. It seems like you have finally found the girl of your dreams."

"No. I mean, they got it all wrong. That girl was not the heiress of the Malhotra group," said Karan.

"Thank God. I despise that pompous Neeru Malhotra. If it's not Lavanya, then who was it?"

"I don't know. They, the Malhotras, introduced me to her as Lavanya. But towards midnight when I removed her…" I paused and Mom choked on her tea. Gosh, that must have sounded weird!

"No, spare me the details of your courtship. Just tell me who she was," Mom blurted out.

"Mom! I was talking about when I removed her mask—the mask she is wearing in this photo. She wasn't Lavanya. I don't know who she was. She ran away when Mrs Malhotra came to the garden."

"You were in the garden with her?" his Mom asked, her voice low, eyes shining as if myriad plans —all arrows in her cerebral flowchart leading to a bubble named 'Karan's marriage'— were being processed at the speed of light.

"Mom, I know what you are thinking. Don't build castles in the air. Yeah, I confess, I liked her very much. We spent close to two hours together just talking and dancing. But as of now, she is just a mystery to me," I confessed.

"A mystery, huh? A mystery you would like to solve or one you wish to forget," asked Mom.

"Of course, I want to find her real identity. But only because she fooled me into thinking that she was someone else. In all probability, she is an actress."

"Ah! Then we should leave it at that. I can see that you really don't have that kind of an interest in her. Sad. I could have tried finding out her real identity if you were interested, you know? I have my ways. But if you want only revenge, I will not waste my sleuthing skills."

I stared at her. A mad surge of hope made my blood thrum. Could she find her for me? Mom was well connected and her gang was like the local Wikipedia. There was absolutely nothing that didn't come under their radar. The more I thought, the more I was reluctant to throw my mystery girl to their mercy. I didn't hate her for the deception, I was just annoyed. And once I got a breathing space from my schedule, I wanted to look for her myself.

"No. Leave her alone. I don't care who she is," I said hastily. I didn't like how swiftly Mom's lips turned up. It was as if that was exactly the answer she had expected from me.

Mothers! She was not going to leave the matter alone. She would use all her skills to find the girl. And hence, I couldn't help but smile as I headed toward the airport. Amsterdam was waiting.

Business meetings had never felt as boring as they were this time. Time dragged. Thoughts about my girl kept interrupting my solitudes.

Unlike usual, I scheduled some time to go sightseeing. I wanted to know why my mystery girl had said she loved Amsterdam. I could easily imagine the bliss that I'd see on her face if she was with me then. And I dearly wished she was with me. The intensity of that wish was mighty overwhelming.

What kind of spell had she cast on me?

There hadn't been a moment when she was away from my thoughts as I wandered through Amsterdam. Even during meetings, I caught myself smiling like a head case when the memory of her lovely face arrived unbidden into my thoughts.

5

CHANDNI

As the day progressed, it was steadily turning into the worst day of my life. The pain and sense of loss I was experiencing were eerily similar to the day I had lost my parents. Though the memory was vague, it evoked the same painful knot in my chest. I had not slept even a wink last night. I had known that Neeru Aunty wouldn't forgive me for the mistake I had committed.

As expected, just when the day dawned, she summoned me into the living room. Neeru Aunty didn't even allow me to utter a word in my defence before shouting out an order.

"Leave the house today itself. I don't intend to give shelter to disloyal people." She was trembling with temper.

"But where will I go?" I asked stunned by her declaration.

"I don't care. Go to hell. Your parents might be waiting for you eagerly," said Neeru Aunty.

"Please, Aunty. Forgive me," I begged. Even though the Malhotras didn't love me, the Malhotra Mansion had been a haven for me. What did I know of the outside world? I had never lived in any place on my own for even a day.

Neeru Aunty ignored me and continued to stare at the day's newspaper. The entertainment section to be specific. As if it held the key to all happiness in the world.

"If not for you, my Lavanya would have been a bride soon. Look how he is looking at you in this photograph. My poor girl!" she said and threw the newspaper at me.

I forgot to breathe when I saw the photo she was referring to. The photo of me dancing with Karan filled one whole page in the entertainment section. My cheeks grew warm reminding me of those magical moments in Karan's company, our dance and those kisses. Moments that had enriched my soul and delighted my heart.

"You. Look here," Neeru Aunty was addressing me now. "Did you tell that boy the truth about Lavanya?"

"No. I didn't."

"Good. At least you did that right. I haven't ever seen anyone as idiotic as you. And as for the scholarship, you will not receive it anymore. That is going to be the punishment for your mistake."

It felt as if Neeru Aunty had pulled the rug from under my feet. Being a management graduate from St. Xaviers would have helped me land a good job. Now that prospect seemed like a distant possibility. I was so close to attaining my dream. I couldn't lose everything now.

I didn't have any money to spare as the Malhotras had never paid for the work I did. According to them, I was, after all, getting free boarding, food and transport. The van that transported some of the staff working at the factory also dropped me to college daily. I prepared the food I ate and she kept a tab on even the smallest extra amount of money they spent on me.

"You already owe me a lot of money. I have it all noted down here," said Neeru Aunty flashing her tiny notebook of accounts. I remembered how she used to write down whenever she gave me money. Even if it was just ten rupees to buy a pen, she would note it down.

What could I do to complete my studies? Maybe I could work as a maid and earn some money. Yes! That could be a solution. I would have to ask around. Someone among the staff might help me find a suitable position.

Neeru Aunty swept out of the room leaving me alone with my thoughts. I pulled out my phone and texted Vani and Shweta. They immediately replied saying they would find a solution. As for now, they were going to come and pick me up.

It took only an hour to gather all my belongings. Everything fit into three medium-sized cloth bags Grandmother had stitched long ago using old curtains. My eyes brimmed with tears when I stopped at the entrance of the Malhotra Mansion and looked back. This was the place where I had grown up. This had been my home all my life.

What would happen to me now? What could I do to survive?

The gardener, the security and the cook, the three people among the staff I was the closest to, came out to see me off. Their faces were grave. They had been like family to me after Grandmother passed away.

"I am quitting too. She can't do this to you. They are so heartless," said Mani, the gardener. The security and the cook also chimed in.

"Hey, don't make any rash decisions. You have mouths to feed. I am sure I will be able to find a new job soon," I said.

While they talked about my possible options, a car slowed down at the gate and stopped near us. Vani and Shweta rushed out.

I had told them what had transpired in the morning, though I had avoided telling them the real reason behind the ouster. If I mentioned it to Vani or Shweta, they would take it out on Lavanya and she would lash back at me. And the campus would become unbearable.

"You can stay with us," said Vani, taking hold of my bag.

Vani and Shweta lived as paying guests in a posh villa in a suburb near my college.

"I can't afford to pay the rent there," I said. All I had was a bundle of hundred-rupee notes that I had found stashed inside an old tin box inside the cupboard. Grandmother's final savings.

"Don't say a word. Who asked you to pay?" said Shweta taking the bag from Vani and placing it inside her car. I had stayed at their place many times before during exams. It was indeed my best option. My eyes misted when I saw their determined faces.

"Thank you, girls, for doing this," I said and we all hugged before getting into the car.

My life as I knew it had ended. A new, unknown phase was beginning. I didn't know how it would phase out. But I had to start somewhere. I let out a deep sigh and leaned back on the car seat. Vani was talking non-stop as Shweta expertly took us through the bumper-to-bumper Mumbai traffic toward their PG accommodation. After listening to them for a while, I zoned out and fell asleep.

When I woke up, we had reached Krishna Vilas. The PG was run by Sugandhi Iyer, a strict Tamil Brahmin woman, who lived on the top floor of the three-storeyed house. She was a widow and took in only single women or students who came with a good reference. Since Shweta and Vani were her pets, she had quickly agreed to let me become a resident.

One of the tenants at the villa, Shweta's distant cousin, Gita, was moving to the US for an on-site for three months. She had been looking for someone to rent the room while she was away. Gita didn't want to let go of her room as it would be hard to get another place like Krishna Vilas once she returned. Before coming to fetch me, Shweta and Vani had convinced Gita to allow me to be her replacement. Also, as Gita had paid for her rent for the three months to reserve the room there wasn't any need to pay anything. Gita was flying to the US the next morning.

I was indeed lucky. As I settled into the room, I raised my head towards heaven in gratitude.

It was as if everything had fallen into place without trying too hard. The Universe truly had my back.

As the night set in, my thoughts inevitably wandered to the night before and to the man who had stolen my heart. Would I ever see him again?

Madhumita Varma's blood boiled as she listened to Rakesh, the young private investigator, briefing her about the latest developments at the Malhotra Mansion. It had not come as a surprise to her that Neeru Malhotra had used an orphan she was supporting to dupe the press and to attract possible suitors for her prodigal daughter. She knew how vile Neeru was. Rakesh had taken a week to investigate before coming to Madhumita with the details.

The fact that Karan had fallen for the poor girl didn't trouble her at all. Love was love. She was pleased to hear that the girl, Chandni, studied in the same college as Lavanya. In fact, according to Rakesh, she had secured the seat on a merit basis. The girl was working at the Malhotra Mansion as a maid to pay for her keep.

"The girl is now staying at a paying guest accommodation called Krishna Vilas PG with her friends," said Rakesh.

This piece of information cheered Madhumita. Sugandhi Iyer, the woman who ran the PG, was a good friend. Their love for Carnatic music and filter coffee had bonded the two women while they had been neighbours in Andheri a long time ago. It was time to give her friend a call.

That afternoon, when Madhumita stepped into the compound of Krishna Vilas, Sugandhi was tackling the weeds in the tiny vegetable garden that she maintained. When she saw her, Sugandhi rushed to wash her muddy hands and greeted her old friend with a huge grin.

"Such a pleasure to see you! What brings you here today?" said Sugandhi giving a bear hug to Madhumita. Madhumita hugged her back and her face lit up with a grin matching that of Sugandhi's.

"How are you, dear?" asked Madhumita.

"I am splendid. Ever since that old man died, I am living life king's size. If I had known this was how it would be when he died, I would have personally sent him off to hell long ago. The scoundrel ate away a third of my good life."

Madhumita snickered. Colonel Subramanian Iyer had been a difficult man and Madhumita had often pitied Sugandhi for her plight. The man had treated her like a slave. Sugandhi had become truly independent and happy after the death of her husband.

"In a way, it was a boon that he was impotent. I don't have to deal with insolent kids who could have inherited all his bad genes." Sugandhi continued to ramble. "Not everyone can expect to have a son as gentle and loving as yours. How is he, by the way? Heard he is in love with that Neeru Malhotra's daughter. You okay with that?"

Madhumita swallowed. Rumours were buzzing that Karan had fallen for Lavanya. She was sure half of it was industrially fuelled by Neeru herself. Clearing her throat, she dismissed it all.

"He is not in love with Lavanya for sure. He denied all the rumours. But I think he has fallen in love with someone. But left to himself, his love will slowly face sudden death. You know how he is. This is the first time that he has shown interest in somebody. That is the reason I came here."

"Here? What do you mean?"

Madhumita led her to the garden bench intending to tell her Karan's little love story.

Just then a girl entered the compound and Sugandhi waved at her.

"Shall we continue this discussion in the kitchen? Poor Chandni seems exhausted. Let me make her some tea. She had three interviews today. By the look on her face, she didn't succeed in any."

This was Chandni? The girl approaching them was lovely. Even though she didn't have a bit of makeup on her skin and was dressed in an old, ordinary kurta and jeans, she looked winsome in every way. Cheap glasses hid her lovely eyes, but they added a nerdy sort of vibe to her heart-shaped face. If without makeup she looked so pretty, she wondered how she must have looked the night of the party, when she had been all dolled up. No wonder Karan had fallen for her.

"I see you have a visitor. You stay and talk with your friend, Aunty. I will make coffee for you both," said Chandni when she saw them.

"You will do nothing of the sort. Go take a quick bath and rest. I will make tea and call you. Will rustle up something to eat as well," said Sugandhi. Even though Chandni insisted she was not tired, Sugandhi wouldn't listen to any of it.

"Okay, as you wish, Aunty. But you'll allow me to help you to prepare dinner, right?"

"If you listen to me and rest for a while."

Chandni walked away after nodding politely at Madhumita. Did girls like her exist in today's generation? No wonder Sugandhi seemed to dote on the girl. Sugandhi had forgotten all about the topic they had been discussing and had launched into praising Chandni.

"I have hosted hundreds of girls here. I have never seen anyone as hardworking and considerate as Chandni. Can you believe Neeru Malhotra is her aunt? Last week, she threw her out without any proper reason. I heard she made Chandni work for free at the mansion in the evening. The poor thing. No wonder the girl was low in spirits when she came here."

"Neeru is her aunt?"

"Yes. In fact, this girl would have been the owner of the Malhotra Group if her parents hadn't died leaving her penniless in a cruel twist of fate."

Sugandhi's words stirred awake an almost forgotten memory inside Madhumita. Memories of a fire, a girl who had fallen asleep in her arms after crying all night and little Karan hugging her saying everything would be alright. Chandni was the daughter of Ram Manohar Khanna, the founder of the erstwhile Venus group? Was this destiny? Chandni and Karan had bonded as kids. She didn't doubt that they would suit each other better now.

This particular train of thought made Madhumita determined to help Chandni.

"You seem to like her very much," Madhumita said.

"You would too if you get to know her. It is hard to come across girls like her nowadays."

"Is she that good?"

"She is. I would have been a proud mom had she been my daughter. Now she seems determined to get a job. By the way, can you help her with that? Something that is not too demanding? She has her final exams coming up soon. I told her to start looking for a job after her exams. She wouldn't listen. Says she cannot continue to be a burden on her friends like this. I even told her she could stay here unpaid. But she wants to be independent."

"I think I can help her. I was looking for someone to help me with my charity projects. My assistant is going on maternity leave next month. What is her subject?"

Her assistant had indeed asked her to look for a replacement though Madhumita hadn't thought of replacing her with someone until this moment.

"She is doing her MBA in Finance. She might be the right candidate for you. I will call her down and you can interview her. The poor thing has run herself down attending job interviews. It will be a great help, Madhu."

"I will do what I can," said Madhumita. This was turning out to be more exciting than her original plan. She had come down to Krishna Vilas only to check the girl out. But now she was getting the chance to get to know her more and possibly play Cupid in her son's love story. Madhumita considered whether she should reveal everything to Sugandhi. Maybe later, if everything turned out well, she would thank her for being the harbinger of happiness to her favourite guest.

Chandni came down within half an hour to help Sugandhi with tea. Madhumita watched as the girl playfully ended Sugandhi's protests and took over frying the onion pakoras Sugandhi had been making for tea time. Even as she worked, she narrated the ordeal of her interviews jovially.

Then, once they had settled down for tea, Madhumita had the pleasure of getting to know more about her. She liked how she didn't utter a word against the Malhotras when asked about her current situation. All she said was that her circumstances had changed and hence she was trying to take charge of her own life.

"Listen, Madhu here runs a few charities and she is looking for an assistant. Would you be interested?" asked

Sugandhi when they had all finished their tea and had sat down to talk.

"What would be the kind of work I'd be expected to do?"

"I need someone to handle my accounts and correspondence. I am pathetic at maths and I have a hard time figuring out how computers work. I also need someone to help me prepare speeches for the functions we host. Do you think you can handle that?"

"I can," said Chandni. There was a sparkle in her eyes.

"I don't have a separate office. I work from home. You will have to live in my home as I might need you at any time of the day. I will arrange accommodation for you in my staff quarters if you are okay with that. It won't be that far from your college also," said Madhumita.

"That would be wonderful. I don't know how to thank you."

"I can't say no to a candidate recommended by my dear friend," said Madhumita. Sugandhi hugged her and thanked her profusely for being so kind.

"Give me your mobile number. I will send you my address."

It was with a big smile on her face that Madhumita left Krishna Vilas thirty minutes later. She had asked Sugandhi to not mention Karan to Chandni.

"She might not feel comfortable if she knows there is a bachelor at home," she had cleverly confessed.

Sugandhi had agreed and said Karan wouldn't even notice such a person had joined his household. Madhumita didn't want that. She would make sure that Karan knew about Chandni's arrival. Everything depended on whether he would recognize her.

CHANDNI

"Ah, the Varma Mansion. You are going for a visit there, *beti*?" asked the elderly auto driver, Karim *Chacha*, when I gave him the destination address. Sugandhi Aunty had called her trusted neighbourhood auto driver to take me to my employer's house. I had travelled in Karim's auto multiple times on my way to various interviews. He insisted I call him *Chacha*, which was Hindi for father's brother.

I liked it when random people addressed me as *beti*, which meant daughter in Hindi. I saw glimpses of my parents in them then. "No, *Chacha*. I am going to work for them."

"Oh, great. They are good people. I have a friend working there. Anthony. He is the head butler there. Mention my name to him and he will become your best buddy there."

"I will, *Chacha*," I said.

Even though I was striving to be calm, I was nervous. This was my first real job. Would I be able to handle the work?

According to Sugandhi Aunty, Madhumita headed many charities and was always busy organising charity programs or attending them.

"But I can guarantee this. She will look after you like her own daughter. She is pure at heart. Nothing like that spoiled

Neeru Malhotra, though she is ten times richer than her."

When I arrived at her mansion, Madhumita was away. But Anthony received me warmly and indeed seemed to be on friendly terms with Karim *Chacha*. The butler's face lit with a smile on seeing Karim *Chacha* and they hugged and clapped each other on their backs like old buddies.

"Keep an eye on her. She is important to me," said Karim *Chacha* to Anthony. I bowed my head at Karim *Chacha*, grateful for the recommendation. My declaration that I could carry my bags myself fell on deaf years and Karim *Chacha* carried them to my accommodation as he bantered with Anthony. They left me in my room to settle down.

"Madam will be back only in the evening. I will come to call you then," said Anthony before he left with Karim *Chacha*.

The room he had shown me into was part of the staff quarters situated on the rear side of the complex. It was separated from the main block of the house by the utility block that housed a library, a gym and a large swimming pool. The house itself was almost four times larger than the Malhotra Mansion. Even then, it strangely felt more welcoming than foreboding. The rooms adjacent to mine were occupied by the chief cook and the other female maids of the mansion. The male servants were given accommodation on the top floor of the same block.

I wished Vani and Shweta were with me as I began this new phase. They had gone home as the study break for the final exams had begun. They had not wanted me to leave Krishna Vilas or accept Madhumita's job offer even though they agreed that the job sounded pretty good. For me, the job had seemed like a Godsend. But it had taken a lot of effort on my part to convince them of the same.

"I know why you are doing it. You are convinced you've become a burden to us. But, idiot, we love you and want to be there for you when you need us. Start with the job after the exams," Shweta had told me and Vani had echoed the same in one of the many conference calls they had made to convince me to not take the job before the exams.

"When will you study for the exams? According to Sugandhi Aunty, your employer is a very busy woman. You won't get any time to study," Vani had argued.

"Who knows if the position will be vacant by the time the exams get over? I can't take that risk. The money she offered is really good. If it becomes difficult, I will quit. I promise I will give my exams priority."

I loved Vani and Shweta equally and was touched by their kindness. But how long could I depend on them? They had already paid my exam fees even though I had saved enough money to pay the fees myself by doing a few freelance content writing jobs. They had insisted I save it for emergencies. Knowing it was useless to argue with them, I had deposited the entire amount into my bank account. Once this job offer had come in, for the first time in my life, I had felt hopeful about my future.

I took out the little Ganesha idol that Grandmother had given me long ago. When I placed it on the little altar in the room, it felt as if the little figurine was assuring me that everything would turn out fine. Unpacking and settling into the room did not take much time as I had only a few belongings. Once it was done, I took a quick shower and lit the small oil lamp in front of my Ganesha. Sitting cross-legged in front of the altar, I prayed for serenity and thanked him for all the blessings he was showering on me. Just as I finished my prayers, a knock sounded on my door. It was Anthony.

"Madam has returned home and wishes to see you," he said.

I grabbed a shawl from the cupboard and draped it over the pink salwar kameez I was wearing, dabbed a bit of Grandmother's cream on my face and arms and followed Anthony. Anthony explained the layout of the house and introduced me to a few other people who worked there as and when we met them. Including me, there were about twenty others—the gardeners, the drivers and the maids—who worked inside the complex. Anthony led me to a spacious living room and asked me to wait.

"Madam is on a call and will join you in a moment," said Anthony and left me alone.

The living room was done in shades of light lilac and cool blue. Comfortable looking armchairs faced an electric fireplace and there were exotic decor pieces tastefully arranged on the mantle. French windows at the other end of the room let in the fading light of the sun. The walls showcased several paintings that I believed were original pieces of art.

I stood up to admire the artwork and forgot to breathe when I reached a particular framed photo. Adorning the wall was an almost life-size version of the photo of me dancing with Karan at Lavanya's birthday party. Whose house was this? My hands trembled as I touched Karan's face in the photograph. Would he be still mad at me?

"They look lovely together, don't they? That is Karan, my son." Madhumita's voice shook me out of the stupor I had fallen into. I swallowed. Did Karan's mom recognize me?

"Who is the girl with him?" I asked tentatively.

"No idea. I initially thought it was Lavanya, as the newspaper proclaimed. But Karan says she was not. I framed and put that up there to taunt my son who refuses to settle down. I wish I knew who the girl was. My son seems to have forgotten all about her and has gone back to chasing business deals instead," said Madhumita and sighed as she looked wistfully at the photo.

"Your son lives here?" I asked as my heart raced.

"Yes. But he is hardly home." Madhumita looked fondly at the photo, then exhaling deeply she turned to me. "Don't worry, he won't bother you in any way. I sometimes wonder if he would notice if I was absent from the house for days together. Come, let me show you my home office. You will be in charge of everything starting today."

I composed myself with difficulty and followed Madhumita to the opposite corner of the home. Her home office was located next to her study.

"This is my favourite place in the house. I am handing it over to you. My former assistant, who is starting her maternity leave soon, will brief you about your work tomorrow."

"Thank you," I managed. My heart was still beating like crazy against my ribs. Would Karan recognise me if he saw me? Would he throw me out then?

"Ah, I think Karan has arrived. Let me see if I can introduce you to him today," said Madhumita, looking out through the side window. A black Mercedes had just entered the compound of the house.

A cold sweat broke all over me. I held onto a nearby chair for support. I flinched when I heard the sound of the car doors shutting.

"Ah, his finance manager is with him. That means he'll be occupied for a while. You can go, Chandni. Will introduce you to him some other time," Madhumita said looking at the middle-aged man who got out of Karan's car. After a second, Karan emerged from the car. My heart skipped a beat.

With great difficulty, I mumbled an okay and rushed out of Madhumita's study. How I managed to reach my room without tripping over something or dashing into somebody, I would never know. Once I locked the door, I leaned against it and breathed heavily.

God, what had I gotten myself into? How would Madhumita react if she knew I was the girl in the photograph?

The romantic in me tried to talk to me about the magic of love and professed that Karan would recognise me and forgive me.

But the sensible sage inside me warned me about the benefits of keeping my identity a secret. For that, I would have to avoid meeting Karan at all costs.

Given some time, he would completely forget me, wouldn't he? I just needed time. After all, he had seen me without my glasses and with lots of makeup on. Chances that he would remember me were almost non-existent. He might be meeting pretty girls every day. Also, as Madhumita ma'am said, he was a busy businessman. Not a college Romeo who had all the time in the world to chase after girls or think about a girl with whom he had spent only a few insignificant hours.

When evening came, I had dinner with the other staff members in the staff quarters' kitchen. I listened to the others talk and was relieved to hear that the family was liked by all of them. Whenever someone mentioned Karan's name, my pulse raced. I wondered how I would behave in his presence if this was my condition at the mere mention of his name.

Raju, Karan's driver, was talking non-stop about his master who was the reason he would become a graduate one day. On Karan's insistence, he was taking night classes and dreamt about working as an officer in the Indian Army one day.

The cook was all praise about how the mother-son duo never fussed about the food she cooked even though there were times she had messed up in epic ways.

The gardener talked about the new fountain and landscaping done in the garden, one of the best private gardens in Mumbai.

By the time I returned to my room, I was wishing I hadn't met Karan at the ball. Then I could have just lived and worked as Madhumita Ma'am's assistant without this tension that had gripped me.

But that wouldn't do. That night was the one thing that made me believe in magic. I adored the man I had met at the party. My only regret was that I had messed it all up. If the circumstance had been different, and if I had been someone with higher social standing, I would have boldly walked in front of Karan and perhaps even proclaimed my love.

As of now, all I could do was pray that Karan had forgotten all about the girl he had met that night. I didn't want him to hate me. I didn't want him to be filled with regret about having wasted his time on a fraud.

And yet, a small part of me wished that he hadn't forgotten me. That he had fallen for the girl he met that day. The probability of that happening was extremely low. But that small part of me believed in the improbable.

KARAN

Proof that Mom hadn't forgotten the mystery girl had become evident the day I returned from Amsterdam. I had found her busy directing Anthony to install a blown up, almost life-sized version of the photo from the newspaper in the far corner of our living room. Facing my favourite chair.

She was incorrigible! I had hidden a smile as I rolled my eyes.

"Don't grudge me my happiness. This photo will stay here until you find yourself a wife," she'd said.

Was that a threat?

I'd walked away with a shrug. I had no objection to having my mystery beauty adorn our living room.

But today, the photo was demanding my attention for some unfathomable reason. I looked up from my file for the nth time and gazed at the photo on the wall. The unease had begun when I'd perceived the subtle scent of *parijats*, the fragrance of my mystery girl, inside my home. The yearning that had gripped my heart had lingered. Parijats were perhaps blossoming in this neighbourhood. There wasn't another explanation for the presence of the scent. But wasn't it a bit early for the blooms? If I remembered right, they flowered between August and December. It was only early February now.

Mother cleared her throat audibly, shaking me out of my reverie. I quickly closed the file and stood up.

"Did I disturb you? You seemed to be dreaming about your Cinderella," said Mother. She was beaming.

"Gosh, Mom! You won't spare a chance to tease me, right?"

"I won't. Have you discovered her real identity?"

"No. I don't think I want to." She seemed better off in my dreams.

"Okay. As you wish. By the way, I have replaced Maya with a new girl. Maya is due next month and the work stress is not good for her."

"Good. I hope the new candidate is efficient."

"I think she is. My old friend Sugandhi recommended her. The girl really needed the job."

"Mom! Did you check her qualifications before you hired her?"

Mother easily fell for recommendations. Maya had given her a lot of headaches initially. Even then, Mother had not bothered to look for another candidate as Maya too had been recommended by another one of her friends. It had taken me hours to tutor Maya on the details about Mother's charities. Maybe I would have to do the same with this girl.

"I did. But wait. I will email you her resume. Check her out yourself. She has not completed her MBA yet, but she is a college topper."

"Okay. I will look at it right now."

My phone pinged with an email in the next minute. I opened the resume and began perusing it. I gave a cursory glance at the girl's photo. A huge pair of glasses obscured half her face. A nerd for sure as indicated by her grades in the first year of MBA. Oh! A rank holder for both, the twelfth board exams and her graduation. But something about the face intrigued me. Had I seen her somewhere? The name did not ring a bell nor did the face. Maybe I should talk to the girl and interview her to make sure Mom hadn't selected the wrong candidate yet again.

"She seems good enough. I will look at her work once she settles into the job. Maybe in a day or two."

"Oh! Leave her alone for now. Her final exams begin tomorrow. I'm not planning to bother her much till the end of her exams."

"Then you should have hired her after her exams."

"Then what would have happened to Maya? She needed rest."

I let out a loud sigh and shook my head. This was exactly what I had expected from my dear mother. By the likes of it, someone must have narrated a sob story and made her hire this girl. This girl, Chandni, certainly could star in a tragedy with her innocent looks. I only wished she deserved the love that was coming her way. Mother often forgot that her staff members were humans capable of deception. But perhaps that was also the reason why they doted on her. Our staff loved working for her.

"By the way, are *parijats* blooming in our compound somewhere?" I asked.

"*Parijats*? Now? Are you dreaming, boy?"

"I don't know. I think I smelled them today. I love their fragrance."

"Aha. I didn't know," Mom said and then she beamed at me again.

Wasn't she acting a little weird today? It was as if she was in the midst of some elaborate scheme. Like she was planning a surprise party or something similar. I wondered what plans were brewing in her mind.

Maybe the *parijats* were the reason that my mystery girl kept me company in my dreams that night. Sometime during the night, as I claimed her lips repeatedly and she melted under my caresses, something woke me up. There was no one beside me. The sense of loss left a knot in my chest. I stretched lazily to release the tension caused by the wound-up desire. Moonlight was streaming into my room and I desired to hold my girl once again in my arms. Wouldn't I see her again?

***

Mumbai, 21 February 2018

The hangover of the dream was still heavy in the morning. I thought about her as I showered and fondly remembered the hours we had spent together the night of the party while having breakfast. And then when I saw my dreamy expression in the mirror as I dressed for the office, I shook my head and ordered myself to snap out of it. I had other important issues to handle. It took me a while to clear my head. Just as I got into the car to leave for the office, Mom called out to me.

"Karan, can you drop Chandni at her college today? She studies at St. Xaviers."

I did not object. The college was on my way. I went back to browsing through my schedule and making notes on my iPad. Was she going to insist I did this daily?

"Chandni, come here. Raju will drop you off. I don't want you to walk there on the first day of the exam."

Raju eagerly opened the front passenger door for Chandni as she approached our car. I glanced up for a moment to see a girl dressed in a light blue churidar get into the car. The moment she got in, Raju began bombarding her with questions.

Had she studied well?

Was she nervous?

Was she confident she would pass?

Chandni answered all of his questions patiently. Raju sounded like this girl fascinated him. I couldn't help but wonder if he was half in love with her already. Interesting! I smiled to myself and continued checking my schedule and highlighting items that I thought should be given priority.

The girl clearly hadn't realized that it was me in the back seat. She was giggling at something Raju had said when the delicious fragrance of the *parijats* hit me. Again. Suddenly all my senses were on full alert. Almost at the same moment, Chandni turned in her seat, looked over her shoulder and our eyes met.

Was it my imagination or had she gone all rigid when I held her gaze? Without acknowledging me, she turned away, sat rather stiffly and began to skim through the notebook she had pulled out from her bag.

I kept holding my iPad but my mind had gone completely blank. I breathed in the fragrance, which by now I was sure emanated from this girl. Memories began bombarding me one after the other. Combined with the delectable fragrance, they came alive and danced in my mind's eye. My eyes wandered to Chandni and a seemingly crazy thought struck me. Could it be? My heart raced as if it liked the idea. It couldn't be. She looked so different.

But the question continued to bother me. Clicking on my email inbox, I opened her resume. Then I zoomed in on her pic. To check if my hunch was correct, I took a screenshot of her photo. Then using the Apple pen, I edited it using graphics software. I roughly drew a mask over her face like the one my mystery beauty had worn. Within minutes, I saw the face of my Cinderella looking up at me. The face that had launched a thousand dreams within me. Satiny soft lips that could tempt any living soul, that heart-shaped face and those liquid brown eyes that had bewitched me.

I was so stunned that I didn't react when the car stopped after a few minutes and Chandni stepped out. I watched her hurry away, exactly in the manner she had run away from me that night. My heart swelled with happiness. I had found her.

How had she ended up inside my home? Most probably, it was all Mom's doing. I chuckled out loud. Wasn't I lucky to have such a devious mother?

Chandni! The name, which meant moonlight in Hindi, suited her perfectly. She had indeed charmed me like a moonbeam, made my heart serenade at the window of her soul. The only reason I hadn't dashed out of the car after her then was because I knew she would be returning to my home. I mentally made a note to come home early today. And I would find her.

I whistled my favourite symphony—Mozart's 25th symphony. Made famous by A. R Rahman after he adapted it into a popular jingle for the Titan watches' advertisement. Raju turned back at me and asked, "You whistle that melody usually after a successful meeting. Have you received some good news?"

"Yes. The best kind."

My day had suddenly turned interesting. I couldn't wait to get back home. I couldn't wait to talk to her again.

Very soon, many other delightful, as well as disastrous, thoughts started to pop up in my mind without delay.

God, how I yearned to taste those lips again!

Once she was in my arms, I was not going to let her go again.

How in the world was I going to drag myself through the day?

The day ahead suddenly seemed so long.

CHANDNI

As I ran toward the examination hall, I wiped my forehead to get rid of the cold sweat that had broken out. That was a narrow escape. Thank you, *Bappa*, for the miracle. Karan had not recognised me. He had been immersed in his work throughout the trip. Sheer luck.

Perhaps not. I was not that memorable a person anyway. He must have forgotten me completely. The thought, though painful, got rid of my anxiety. Yes, I was being paranoid for no reason. Karan would never associate me with the beauty he saw at the party.

It was hence with a smiling face that I met Vani and Shweta. As was our custom, we began discussing probable questions. By the time the exam began, my confidence was back and all unnecessary anxieties had vanished. I could answer most of the questions and I emerged from the examination hall confident of scoring a good grade in exam.

As I waited for my friends to emerge from the examination hall, fears started to command my attention again. What if, by bizarre chance, Karan remembered me? What if he outed me to his mother? Wouldn't I lose my job? I couldn't afford that to happen. I had to find a way to remain unseen.

On second thought, I realized that, in that big house, it was not such a task. I knew that Karan came home only after six in the evening or sometimes even later. I had to just ensure that I left the house by then and returned to my room. Yes, that would be easy. Or should I start staying with Vani and Shweta again? But Madhumita Ma'am wanted me to stay at her home as my services might be needed at any time during the day. So, I couldn't stay away from the Varma Mansion.

Madhumita Ma'am had asked me to prioritize my exams as of now. Maya would be completing the projects she had started and would also be helping me learn the ropes.

What if Karan returned home unexpectedly and recognised me? This time our eyes had met only for a second or so. If we spent more time with each other, something might trigger recognition. As each second passed, paranoia started to tighten its grip on me. Maybe I could leave the mansion in the evening and stay at Krishna Vilas for the duration of the exams stating group study as an excuse. I could finish my duties by then hopefully. I didn't know if Madhumita Ma'am would agree but I had to give that a shot.

After we finished analysing the question papers and having concluded that all three of us were going to pass with flying colours, Vani and Shweta began to question me about my job.

"What? You are working for Madhumita Varma? Karan Varma's mother? The Karan Varma?" screamed Vani.

"Oh my God. Can I be your assistant?" asked Shweta.

I chuckled. If only they knew the tension I was going through. I was still uncertain if I could share my secret with them. I wanted to, but should I? It was, in a way, Lavanya's secret.

"Tell me, is he as gorgeous as he appears in his photos? How tall?"

"I came in his car today as Madhumita Ma'am asked him to drop me. He was glued to his iPad the whole time and ignored me completely," I shared truthfully.

"Oh, God! You lucky girl. I would barter anything in the world to breathe the same air as him. Maybe you can invite us there for group study," said Vani dreamily.

"You must be joking. My accommodation is separate. I live in the staff quarters. I was about to ask if I could crash with you both till the exams got over."

"But why? With Karan around, I would never want to leave the compound. You can bump into him accidentally, you know," said Shweta with a wink.

My cheeks grew warm. Wouldn't that be nice? Their words brought back sweet memories.

"Look at her. She is blushing. If Karan saw you now, he would fall head over heels in love with you."

"As if! Be serious. Can I come to Krishna Vilas for a group study like I always did? I miss you both," I asked. Studying with them was always fun. At the mansion, my thoughts would wander, affecting my studies.

"Of course, you can. But if I were you, I wouldn't even think about leaving the premises. Who knows! Karan Varma might fall for the nerdy, beautiful girl with Bambi's eyes," said Vani.

I rolled my eyes. Fat chance.

"Can you girls come with me now? I will introduce you to Madhumita Ma'am. Maybe you can talk to her about the group study?"

"Of course. I hope Karan is at home," said Vani fluttering her eyelashes. I swatted her arm. She looked at me with a pout. This girl!

Vani and Shweta were fascinated by everything around them the moment we entered Varma Mansion. Perhaps due to the awe that my employer inspired in them, they held off voicing any silly declarations or wishes the entire time that we spent there. Thankfully, Madhumita Ma'am was okay with the group study idea when I mentioned it.

"There is nothing major scheduled for the next few weeks. Only a few small functions. You can help me with them during the day. Stay with them and do well in your exams," she told me as she treated us to tea and snacks. She even asked me to show them around the house. My friends emerged from the Varma Mansion two hours later all dreamy-eyed and subdued. They remained silent all the way back to Krishna Vilas.

"I tell you, I can kill to be the daughter-in-law of your Madhumita Ma'am," said Shweta as we finally sat down at Krishna Vilas with our thick textbooks to study for the next exam.

"Me too. God, she is so nice. I envy that bitch Lavanya who was in that photo with Karan. The way he was looking at her! I might just die if he looked at me that way," said Vani.

This time, I blushed furiously. Glimpses of his ardour bubbled up in my mind's eye.

"Girls, concentrate. You can both swoon over my employer's son once the exams get over. Do you hear?" I said, swatting Vani's shoulder with her notebook.

"Ugh! You are such a party pooper. Who wants to be reminded of mergers, acquisitions & corporate restructuring when one can dream about dancing the night away in the arms of a billionaire?" declared Vani dreamily. We all laughed together.

Their comments gave food to my thoughts. The girl who would end up with Karan would truly be lucky. Of course, that could never be me. I was never lucky. If I was, I would have been born in a household like that of Lavanya or Vani or Shweta. But with what was my reality, Madhumita Ma'am would never even consider me as a prospective bride for Karan. And Karan had surely forgotten me.

Sugandhi Aunty brought black coffee laced with butter saying it would give us energy. While I sipped the coffee gratefully, she asked about how my job was.

"I knew you would love it. Remember that you can trust Madhumita. Give her this when you return. She used to love my pickles," she said placing a huge jar of pickled mangoes on the table in the room. "Our men bonded over alcohol. It was our love for good food that cemented our friendship. I cooked for her and she would take me to the fanciest restaurants to taste exotic dishes that we would later try to recreate together in our kitchens. Those days were so much fun. It all stopped when her husband passed away. She had to take over many responsibilities as Karan was studying. He was a wild child then. The trauma of losing his father changed him," said Sugandhi Aunty.

"Wild child? Really? How wild?" asked Vani, keeping her coffee aside. Shweta finished her coffee all at once and sat cross-legged on her bed eager to hear Karan's tales. Strangely, I was not ready to hear anything about his unrestrained side. As if she had read my thoughts, Sugandhi Aunty refused to divulge Karan's secrets.

"Study. Gossip won't help you pass the exam."

No amount of cajoling changed her stance.

"You are such a tease. Dangling the carrot and then asking to forget about it," complained Vani.

"I didn't know you liked carrots. When did I do that anyway? Go study, girls, instead of poking around for trouble. Your parents will have my neck if you fail."

"Not mine. They have told me that they don't care if I fail or pass. After all, they love their would-be-son-in-law."

Shweta was already engaged to be married to a family friend's son. Even though their parents had set them up, the two had clicked from the moment they met. She was to be married at the end of the year.

Sugandhi Aunty left muttering to herself that she was glad she was childless. Because she would have murdered them if her kids had turned out to be like us.

Wild! That one word kept me company throughout the evening. My thoughts darted often toward the one who had forgotten me. Had I encountered that person at the party that day? Was that why Karan hadn't recognised me? I had seen how Lavanya lived her life. And I had heard enough tales. Booze, men, drugs. Nobody could beat her when it came to craziness.

The man I remembered from the party hadn't seemed like someone who was in her league. Karan had never been mentioned in any scandal as far as I knew, whereas Lavanya was almost always plunging into one or the other scandal.

Karan had won me over with his undeniable charm. I doubted if I would ever find another man who would have that kind of effect on me. I was certainly destined to become a spinster.

Sometimes, it was best to leave things in the hands of destiny. If things weren't supposed to happen the way I wanted, I preferred to believe that Ganapati Bappa had a better plan in store for me. He hadn't given me cause to distrust him till now. The only advice Grandmother used to repeat was to trust Bappa unconditionally. I firmly believed that the one who removed obstacles from the lives of millions of devotees would have my back. He would guide me back to the right path even if I strayed for a while, chasing mirages.

True love was probably just that—a mirage. How many true love stories did I even know?

How could I blindly seek it knowing that it might vanish in a flash?

But then, wasn't a life devoid of love akin to a barren desert? The oasis of love meant something even though it existed only in the mind of the dreamer. Something to cherish, something magical.

My tiny oasis of love taught this deluded orphan to dream and hope. And wasn't hope an audacious thing? It refused to give up even when everything was falling apart.

10

KARAN

"Where is Chandni? I have time today to instruct her," I asked settling into Mother's chair in her study.

"She is not here. She's gone to her friends' place to prepare for tomorrow's exam. I gave her permission to do so."

It would have been the understatement of the year to say I was disappointed. All through the day, I had been looking forward to spending time with Chandni. I had even mentally prepared a script as to how I would let her know that I had finally found her. Was it just bad timing or was she avoiding me?

"But then who will take care of your work?"

"Maya has agreed to take charge if anything comes up at night. As of now, I haven't committed to anything major for the next two weeks. Chandni can easily handle them. Our yearly trip to Lonavala is the only thing that we have scheduled after that."

I had forgotten all about the yearly outing we arranged for our staff. Every year, in the first week of March, we took the staff on a leisure trip to Lonavala. We usually stayed at the resort I owned there and engaged in the same kind of activities every year. In a way, it was utterly boring and predictable. But still, our staff looked forward to the trip every year.

This time though, I had reasons to look forward to it. Unlike before, there was one member of our staff that I wished to spend more time with. Maybe it was time to make some new plans. I had two weeks to prepare for it. Two weeks would pass in the blink of an eye, given my busy schedule.

Yet my foolish heart hoped I might get a chance to meet Chandni sooner than that.

The fact that Chandni was avoiding me became clear by the end of the week. Every day of the first week, Chandni left home before I returned from the office. If she could play this game, so could I.

From then on, I began to stay late at the office. On the first day of the second week, I announced to Mother that I was leaving on a trip to Delhi. I casually mentioned that I would be away for at least three days.

As expected, when I called Mother from Delhi the next day, I learned that Chandni hadn't gone for the group study but was, in fact, studying on her own. I booked a return ticket immediately and landed in Mumbai in the early hours of the next morning.

My heart raced just at the thought of seeing her again.

What would be her reaction?

Would she run away again?

I couldn't risk that. I couldn't lose her again. Maybe I shouldn't seek her out. I should continue to act as if she was a stranger. Yes, that was the only way. But I soon realized that the temptation to be near her, to see her, to talk to her, to hear her voice was stronger than my willpower to take it slow.

I could accidentally bump into her, couldn't I? That seemed like a good idea.

So, I headed to the pool for an early morning swim. I knew that my presence in the pool would be noticeable from Chandni's room. As I swam across the pool, I stealthily eyed her windows. A curtain quickly closed the next time I looked in that direction during a break between laps. I couldn't help but smile. She would have panicked when she realized it was me. I was curious about what tactics she would employ to stay clear of me today. I continued to swim but kept checking for any movements from her room. The curtains remained closed, much to my disappointment.

Did she think that I would expose her deception if I recognised her? Was that the reason she was avoiding being in my presence?

The more I thought about it, the more I was convinced that might indeed be the case. My princess was afraid of me. That was a depressing thought. After completing my usual twenty laps, instead of hurrying to get ready for the office like usual, I found myself lounging on a pool chair lost in thoughts.

How could I convince her that I didn't want answers, that I wasn't about to question her actions? Destiny had made us meet and I had fallen head over heels in love with her. Why was fate putting obstacles in my path now?

Chandni didn't emerge from her room even though it was almost time for her to leave for her exams. Was she that scared of me? I stood up and walked towards the poolside shower, slightly disgruntled. Anthony came to inform me that Mother was waiting for me at the breakfast table.

After showering, I changed out of my wet clothes and donned a fresh pair of track pants and a T-shirt. Just as I was about to proceed to the main house, I saw Chandni hurrying out of her room carrying her books and bag. She was looking around as if she dreaded that I might suddenly appear in front of her from some direction. Maybe I should prove her fears right!

I stood waiting near the library for her to approach. When she stepped into the corridor in front of the library, which led towards the house, I walked directly into her path. For an onlooker, it would have appeared as if I had just strolled out of the library. Chandni almost collided with me before stopping herself with a tiny yelp.

"Careful, girl. Look where you are going." I perused her from head to toe as if I was seeing her for the first time. My poor little darling had become as pale as a sheet of paper. Enjoying the turmoil I was causing, I continued casually, "You must be mother's new assistant. What's your name?"

Her eyes widened slightly but colour slowly started to return to her face.

"Yes, Sir. I'm Chandni," she mumbled.

"Good to finally meet you, Chandni. Heard a lot of good things about you from Mother," I said, extending my hand toward Chandni.

"Honoured to meet you, Sir," said Chandni, shaking my hand.

Honoured indeed! More like scared out of her wits. Her hand was trembling inside my palm. I let go of her hand to end her distress.

"Don't you have an exam today?" I asked, taking care to keep my tone soft and comforting.

"Yes, Sir. I was on my way."

"Do well in the exams. Ask Raju to drop you. Best of luck," I said with a smile and walked toward the house. Was that a sigh of relief that I heard? I chuckled inwardly. There! I had convinced her that I had not recognized her at all. Now perhaps she would stop running away from me.

Mom was waiting for me at the breakfast table with an ear-to-ear grin. Time to put on my acting shoes again. Surely, she was expecting me to confess that my love for Chandni had brought me back to Mumbai earlier than expected.

"My work got wrapped up early. So good to be back home," I said, sliding into a chair next to Mother and helping myself to some hot parathas. "Ah, *gobi parathas*. Just what I was craving for."

Mother passed the bowl of curd to me. "So, there was no other reason for your abrupt return?"

"What other reason? By the way, I met your assistant a little while ago. What was her name? Ah, Chandni."

Mother's eyes widened. She hadn't seen that coming, had she?

"You met Chandni? And?"

I wanted to hug her. My dear old mother badly wished to hear that I had recognised Chandni. But she was in for some short-term disappointment. "And what else? She was hurrying to college and I wished her the very best for her exams."

I continued to eat my breakfast silently trying hard to unsee the disappointment on Mother's face. I badly wanted to come clean to her. But hadn't she brought this upon herself? She was the one who kept the identity of my girl a mystery until now. This was fun. So much better than me dancing to her tunes. Ha! I fully intended to see my charade through to the end.

In the evening, I guided Chandni through the details of how our charities functioned. I introduced her to the software we used and guided her through the lessons donning my cool-boss avatar. In truth, it wasn't easy at all.

I had encountered and survived multiple moments where I wanted to snatch Chandni into my arms and stun her with a passionate kiss.

There were instances when her proximity made me go breathless.

And there was that one time when I almost confessed.

But in each of those weak moments, I fought valiantly against every untoward desire. And succeeded.

When all I could see were her lips, I closed my eyes and counted backwards from a thousand.

When I had to lean closer to show her the relevant tabs in our banking software, I concentrated on recalling everything I had learned about it. She might have tagged me as an emotionless and unintelligent being like Alexa when I uttered useless details like 'This tab opens up the about section of this software and tells us when it was created. It cannot be edited.'

Slowly and with continued effort over the following days, Chandni began to relax in my company. My acting must have been superlative because she no longer flinched when we met unexpectedly (quite frequently, if I may add) in the corridors of the house. Our rapport improved so much that Chandni no longer ran to Krishna Vilas for group studies and was okay with me dropping her to college on my way to the office.

We chatted about mundane things sometimes and I loved hearing her wise answers. We were creating new memories and I devoted myself to peeling off the layers of her resistance. In the process, I was falling helplessly in love with each hour that passed in her company. Every cell in my being bloomed when I heard her laughter. A casual touch could kindle a thousand desires.

By the end of the month, my patience was vanishing like the morning mist in the presence of the sun's rays. I craved more than a casual acquaintance with my girl. Yet, I knew it was not yet time. I still couldn't see the ardour I wished to see in Chandni's eyes. Wouldn't she fall in love with me? I was almost despairing that I couldn't find reasons to be closer to her anymore once I completed training her when something unusual happened.

They say memories are timeless treasures that our heart stores deep within for us to discover when the time is right. One such memory peeked out unexpectedly on the day of the Lonavala trip giving me more reasons to believe that Chandni was destined to be in my life.

All the staff had been jolly and jubilant once we reached the resort that morning. They were to go on a short trek, have a picnic at a picturesque viewpoint on the hills and then, once they returned to the resort, they would have dinner and spend time singing and dancing around a bonfire.

I had decided to just stay at the resort managing some urgent work remotely. I watched as they left the resort all excited and loud like a bunch of school kids. I would have continued working peacefully and finished my pending work if I hadn't seen Raju escorting Chandni. He was walking closer to her than was necessary and had a goofy grin on his face. After fidgeting around without doing anything for half an hour, I quickly changed into a tracksuit and pullover and followed them.

It took me an hour to finally reach the spot where they had gathered for the picnic. To my disappointment, I couldn't find Chandni in the group. Nor could I spot Raju. I seethed inwardly. Was my driver going to be my nemesis?

"Where did Chandni go? I need her help with something I am working on," I said to the cook who seemed surprised by my sudden appearance.

"She went for a walk. She said she wanted to check if the Rajmachi Fort was visible from the viewpoint over there."

To my relief, I saw Raju carrying the lunch baskets to the clearing nearby. With a smile playing on my lips and happily whistling Mozart's 25th symphony, I walked in the direction the cook had indicated.

My heart lurched when I finally spotted Chandni. She was standing atop a narrow boundary wall that overlooked a cliff. Was she about to jump? With my heart in my mouth, I dashed towards her and pulled her into my arms.

"Don't even think about it," I shouted, gathering her in a tight embrace. And just like that, I remembered a similar scene from years ago.

Chandni was that girl! That girl whom I'd met when I had gone to give a talk at a college in the city. That girl whose sad eyes had haunted my waking moments for days. My fingers tightened around her arm. No wonder I had felt the need to protect her whenever she was near.

I held her close, listening to her breathe. Just grateful for the fact that she was alive.

"Sir, let me go. What happened?" Chandni asked, pushing me away.

"You were about to jump, weren't you?" I asked, angry that she valued her life so little.

"Jump? No. Even if I jumped, nothing would have happened. See, the ground on the other side of this wall is at the same level as this side. The cliff begins a few metres away from this wall."

I checked and what she said was indeed true. I was at a loss for words. How could I explain my action? I had no reason to hug an employee.

"You are that girl, the girl on the ledge. You were about to jump off a ledge that day too, weren't you? No wonder you seemed so familiar." I pointed out.

Chandni blushed. This time surely with embarrassment.

"That was so long ago! You remember me?" she asked.

"Rescuing you was my first and only act as a superhero. How can I forget that? You seem to have a suicidal tendency. I should keep a constant watch on you from now on," I said.

"I wasn't about to jump off," she said.

"Who knows," I teased, now convinced that she was speaking the truth.

For the rest of the day, I made jibes at her whenever possible and even threatened to narrate the incident to the staff during the bonfire that night when we usually shared funny stories.

"Please don't tell them. They will make my life hell. I will do anything you say," she said when the bonfire was about to begin.

Anything? Did she even know what all I could make her do? My dirty mind immediately travelled at breakneck speed to many scandalous destinations though I valiantly put a rein on its mad escapades.

Instead, I decided to keep her beside me late into the night by making her sort a folder containing more than a thousand photos of our farm products. She was to create separate folders for the vegetables and fruits. While the rest of the staff danced the night away, we sat on the opposite ends of a table in the common room engrossed in our work.

Chandni might have fried me alive if she knew that the said folder contained photos from five years ago and had been long discarded. But she wouldn't ever know, would she?

11

CHANDNI

I should have felt relieved that Karan hadn't recognized me. But strangely, that was not the emotion that became my constant companion after the trip to Lonavala. Yes, I still worried he would hate me if he realized I was the one who'd tried to deceive him.

It was sheer torture to be with him now. He lost no opportunity to tease me on every possible occasion. He treated me like a difficult kid who had to be kept under constant vigilance.

The real problem was that I could never be at ease when he was around. My mind went numb if I ran into him unexpectedly in the house. My pulse raced even if he simply looked at me. In those moments, I longed for the man who had made my toes curl with his ardour. Was he the same person who had kissed me like my lips were the air he couldn't breathe without?

Even though there were no displays of affection, I couldn't help but fall more deeply in love with him every passing day. It was impossible not to love him.

Other staff members at the house had only praises reserved for him whenever he became a topic of discussion during dinner, which was almost every day. Sometimes, I found him joking with Raju or the gardener and hugging them or patting their backs as if they were his equals. I couldn't recollect any such thing ever happening at the Malhotra household. Their servants were treated almost like slaves and were often reminded of their station via deriding comments.

Mornings these days began in the same manner. I would sit near my window when he swam in the pool in the morning and ogle at him shamelessly. Looking like a Greek God, he would lounge on the poolside chair after his swim and sinful thoughts would accost me. I would wonder how those perfectly sculpted abs would feel under my palm and my body would heat up. Breathing deeply to ward off those thoughts, I would pray to Bappa for redemption from my sins and move away from the window. Yet, I would return to my window seat the next day the moment I heard his dolphin-like body splashing around in the pool.

Karan had gifted me a Parker pen as a good-luck charm to write my exams on the day he'd returned from Delhi. When I showed it to the others during dinner, Raju had taken out a similar one Karan had gifted him when he wrote his tenth board exams. All my happiness had whooshed out like air from a deflating balloon. Like a fool, I had thought he was beginning to like me. Obviously, he treated all his staff equally.

Now that my exams had ended, I was going to be deprived of the time I could spend with him in his car. I was already comfortable handling the accounts, so there wouldn't be any more accounting lessons either. Maybe there would be other occasions.

A few days later, while I was at the house discussing an event detail with Madhumita Ma'am, I noticed Karan staring wistfully at our photo in the living room. My chest constricted and I almost ached to tell him the truth. But my old fear popped up again and I fled from the room.

Maybe it was time to stop behaving like a scared mouse and act exactly like how I felt. It was not a crime to be poor. It was not a crime to fall in love with someone like Karan. And he had known I was not Lavanya. The emotion I'd seen on his face as he looked at our photo wasn't hatred. It was evident he still liked the girl he had met that night at the party; there was no other explanation for his fond gaze. The only thing I had to confirm was whether he would like me in real, without the charm of the makeup, the designer clothes and an elevated social standing.

Would he fall for someone like me?

The probability of that happening was very low. Yet, I wanted to hang onto any tiny thread of hope that I could find. Also, I wanted to own my truth, no matter what the consequence. I wanted to take my chances.

So, one evening, I took extra care to dress, applied kajal in my eyes and dabbed Grandma's cream for added confidence when Madhumita Ma'am called me to take care of a few urgent correspondences. If my luck was good, Karan would be home and I might see his handsome face once again.

I was greeted by the sound of laughter upon entering the house. Curious, I peeked into the living room on my way to the study and froze. Sitting on the couch with her hand lingering possessively on Karan's shoulders was the prettiest girl I had ever seen. Dressed in a figure-hugging white lace top and blue jeans, her silky hair spilt like dark rainy clouds down her shoulders, she was leaning against Karan and laughing at whatever joke he had cracked. My stomach churned. Had I manifested her through my fears?

"That is Sanvi. Our former neighbour and Karan's best friend. How happy they look together!" exclaimed my employer from behind me causing me to jump back a step. "Oops, I am sorry. Did I frighten you? You look so pale."

"No. No, I am okay," I muttered, trying hard to compose myself. The man I had dreamed about surely seemed out of bounds completely for me now.

"Great. Let's not disturb their happy bubble. Work summons," said Madhumita Ma'am.

Was it my imagination or was Madhumita Ma'am a notch happier than usual? Perhaps the reason was Sanvi's arrival.

The next hour dragged on painfully as sounds of laughter from the living room drifted into the study. I penned boring emails, entered data in spreadsheets and sorted photographs to create a PowerPoint presentation for the charity foundation.

I wondered what they were talking about. I envied their togetherness. Never had so many errors crept in while I typed and never had I felt so miserable. It was as if I was standing on the banks of a river watching a flash flood come in. How long would it take for it to drag me under its swirling waters?

Deep breathing helped, and so did the cup of coffee the cook brought in. Madhumita Ma'am was talking non-stop to her friend on the phone as I worked. Mostly about Sanvi. Unlike usual, her voice disturbed me. There were moments when I felt I might burst out crying and make a fool out of myself. What would my employer think if that happened? I needed to go out and breathe some fresh air. Yes, that was the only thing that would help. So, once I finished my work, I got up to leave.

"Wait. I'll introduce you to Sanvi. She is such a sweet girl," said Madhumita Ma'am. I swallowed as something akin to jealousy frothed within me.

When we entered the living room, my mind blanked out because exactly at that moment I saw Sanvi leap into Karan's arms. Pressing a quick kiss on Karan's cheeks, she declared, "I am the happiest girl in the whole world now. All because of you." Karan chuckled and fondly gazed at her.

Madhumita Ma'am cleared her throat and they turned to look at us. Sanvi blinked in surprise, then ran towards her and hugged her tight. There were tears in her eyes when she declared, "Aunty, Karan is finally making my dream come true. I am going to be the happiest bride in the whole wide world!"

I felt dizzy as Karan's mom congratulated Sanvi warmly. My gaze wandered to Karan's face which still held the remnants of happiness from minutes ago. With a smile, he approached us and stood near Sanvi who was still chattering away about her wedding plans. I quickly looked away ignoring the heaviness in my chest.

"Sanvi, I forgot to introduce you to my assistant. This is Chandni and as I said, she has become quite indispensable to me."

Sanvi beamed as she shook hands with me.

"Good to meet you finally, Chandni. Heard a lot about you from Aunty. You are prettier than I was told."

"Congratulations to both of you. You make an adorable pair," I said, still avoiding Karan's eyes. Tears began to prick behind my eyes. I knew I had to escape before I did something as idiotic as bursting into tears in front of them.

Excusing myself, I fled from there. As my heart silently shattered into pieces, I stumbled on the corridor carpet, fumbled with the main door handle and escaped into the garden. Slumping onto the garden bench, I scolded myself. I was being foolish.

This day had to come anyway. How had I forgotten?

As thoughts crowded inside my mind, I looked around to find solace in the picturesque scenery around. This was one of my favourite places in the complex, the place where I often came to dissolve my fearful thoughts or indulge in lucid dreaming.

Like always, there was a nip in the evening air. Crickets were busy calling out to mates from the nearby bushes. A faint scent of jasmines wafted near and I greedily inhaled the pleasant fragrance. I implored the sound of flowing water from the fountain at the corner of the garden to calm my racing heart. As if to heal me, tears began to flow unhindered. And then, even though I tried to stop it, I began to sob uncontrollably.

Unrequited love was agonizing, especially since this was my first love. Karan had made my heart blossom. Like any besotted fool, I'd weaved dreams around him even though every single atom in my being had screamed to rein it in. But, naive as I was, I had let it waltz me into fantasies. Into dreams that would never come true.

12

KARAN

I stared at the door through which Chandni had disappeared, unable to comprehend what had just happened. How in hell had she got the idea that I was getting married to Sanvi? She was the last person in the world who should believe that I was tied to someone else. Yes, I was ready to be chained to someone for life. To Chandni. No one else. I had to go after her and clear the misunderstanding.

"Did your assistant just congratulate me and Karan?" asked Sanvi incredulously to Mom, "Who can even think about that? Engaged to this monkey? Ridiculous!"

"You wound me. You say it as if I am an odious creature. I should go," I said, as I turned and strode towards the main door to go after Chandni. Sanvi followed and stopped me.

"Do you know who quickly jumps to such ridiculous assumptions about you?" she asked.

"Who?"

"An idiot... or someone who is helplessly in love with you," whispered Sanvi with a twinkle in her eye.

My brows wrinkled as I contemplated it. Could it be? Had my Cinderella fallen in love with me? She hadn't given me any reason to think so. She always escaped from my vicinity as quickly as she could.

A full-blown smile had now taken over Sanvi's face.

"My, my! I didn't think I would live to see this day. You are in love!"

"I didn't say I wasn't," I said as a grin appeared on my face. Mom was near me the next moment.

"So, you recognised her?" Mom was rubbing her palms together in satisfaction.

"Of course."

"When? How? I was despairing that you wouldn't recognise her at all," Mom asked eagerly.

"You underestimated me, Mom. I recognised Chandni the day you made me give her a lift."

"I am so glad that trick worked," said Mom.

All this while, Sanvi was staring at us with her hands on her hips trying to understand our conversation. At this point, she lost her patience and barged in, "Can you both stop speaking in code and explain what this is all about? What are you talking about?"

"Long story," I said.

"Make it short," demanded Sanvi.

"Later," I said and headed toward the door again.

"Now. Or I might die from anxiety."

"I pity poor Ashutosh. I wonder if he is aware of the peril he is inviting into his life," I teased as Sanvi stubbornly followed me.

"Oh, he knows what a lovely life awaits him. But if you don't tell me your story now, I am going to make your life miserable," threatened Sanvi.

"Let him go. I will tell you," said Mom.

"No, Aunty. I want him to tell. He hid such a big secret from me. He should pay the price. Is that girl truly your girlfriend? You were both acting as though you barely know each other."

"I wish she was my girlfriend. She is not, yet. If you will let me, I need to remedy that ASAP."

"Ah! The plot deepens. Spit it out Karan, or else your would-be girlfriend will know about all your flaws."

"You are incorrigible. Come here," I said and dragged Sanvi to the framed photo in the living room. "I will make it short. That is my dream girl, my Cinderella and I met her at a ball. We got separated and Mom somehow found her and employed her. I need to go find her now and tell her that I am not getting married to you. Okay?"

Sanvi gazed at the photo with her eyes wide open. But she turned and stopped me again as I attempted to walk away.

"That makes everything even more intriguing. But why are you so desperate to go to her now. Weren't you both acting as though you were strangers minutes ago?"

"She is pretending as though we have not met and I am pretending that I didn't recognise her."

"Obviously. But don't you think she might be relieved that you are out of her way? I would have rejoiced if it was me in her place," said Sanvi, a mischievous smile dancing on her lips.

"You, brat! Go plan your wedding. Haven't I made your dream locale available for you after pulling some very deft strings? Or should I call and cancel the booking?"

"Oof. Go. Go to your girl," said Sanvi. But just when I took a step toward the door, she stopped me again.

"Are you going to go and tell her that you are her prince charming? And that you are not going to marry this wicked princess?" said Sanvi batting her eyelashes playfully.

"Yup. That's exactly what I am going to do," I said.

"Tell me this. Has she confessed to you that she loves you? Or acted in any way that made you believe that she loved you?" asked Sanvi.

"No," I said. The truth that Chandni had never expressed an interest in me was indeed debilitating. Chandni had started to relax in my company only after I made it apparent that I hadn't recognised her.

"Then make her confess. She is surely in love with you. She looked crestfallen when she congratulated us. Is there something that makes it difficult for her to love you?"

"I don't know. I spent the happiest hours of my life in her company that night. I want her to be mine. But she avoids me like she doesn't care about me at all."

"Okay. Listen. Tell me all about her. It is not a good idea to go behind her now. Let her think you are mine. When we fear losing somebody we love, we become ready to take risks. Do you get me?"

"No. I don't want her to face any kind of stress because of me. I only want to make her happy. I will go to her now and clear all misunderstandings."

"Patience, you idiot. Something that is forbidden becomes a temptation by default. I am sure she'll fall harder for you if we continue with this 'I-am-getting-married-to-you' charade a while longer. Trust me, I know how a female mind works better than you," said Sanvi.

Mom, who had been silent all along, chuckled. She looked at me and said, "Maybe you should listen to her. I am sure Chandni will fall for whatever Sanvi is planning."

"If Aunty thinks we should play this charade, we should," said Sanvi, showing a double thumbs up to Mom.

"Okay. I will not tell her today. But if you make her miserable in any way, you will have to deal with my anger."

"Come with me then. Show me that new fountain in your garden. I heard it changes colours at night."

"It does. I love it, especially during moonlit nights."

Sanvi scoffed. "I can understand why you like moonlight now." Then she teased me by singing *'Chandni…O meri Chandni.'*

"Shut up," I said as we stepped into the garden. The brat continued to sing the popular Bollywood song to rile me.

"Wow! It is so lovely and peaceful here," said Sanvi as she looked around.

As we strolled along the garden path toward the fountain, I noticed the figure sitting on the garden bench near the fountain. A warmth gripped my heart. Chandni was sitting at the exact spot on the bench I loved to sit in. But when I looked closely, I perceived that she was sniffing and wiping her nose. Her shoulders were slumped in defeat. My heart squeezed. The sudden urge to go and comfort her made me take a step toward her.

Just then, Sanvi raised her voice and said, "It is as lovely as I imagined. This fountain is exactly like how I wanted it to be." She also gripped my arm and moved closer to me.

Her sound made Chandni turn toward us. She froze as she spotted us. Even though I couldn't see her face, her stance indicated that she was in agony. Automatically, I took another step toward her.

Sanvi pushed ahead of me and ambled toward Chandni dragging me along, "Is that you, Chandni? Karan was showing me the fountain he constructed as a memento for our love."

I glared at her. A memento of our love? The girl was crazy. The fountain had been Mom's idea. I had played no role in its construction or planning.

Chandni stood up and bowed slightly. "Sorry for intruding. I will go now."

"Oh, forget about it. I don't mind at all. Nor would Karan. You wouldn't. Right, love?" asked Sanvi.

Chandni's eyes were red and puffed. She must have been crying. But she was continuing to avoid meeting my eyes. Maybe I should play the charade that Sanvi had initiated and see if she would confess.

"No, I don't mind," I said, looking straight at Chandni. She stiffened for a second but again mumbled apologies and scampered away from the garden as quickly as possible. I gazed at her as long as she remained in my line of sight.

"My, my. I am loving this," said Sanvi, "Karan, the one with an iron heart, is now helplessly in love. Who knew!"

"I am going to kill you right now. That is what I want to do now."

"And I am going to make her confess her love for you within three days. Want to bet?"

"No. I don't want you to make her more miserable."

"Oh! I plan to make her so desperately in love with you that you will thank me for all that I did!"

I shrugged and walked away from her even as Sanvi complained loudly about abandoning her so heartlessly. Jest or not, I was going to make sure that Sanvi did not end up hurting Chandni.

13

CHANDNI

I knew it wasn't prudent to pine over something that was never destined to be mine. Yet, I was going crazy thinking about Karan. If I had a rupee for every time I thought of him, I would have become a multi-billionaire by now.

I flicked through the many invoices that were to be entered into the company accounts but saw nothing but blank sheets. I should concentrate. The cause of my temporary blindness seemed to be my suddenly-acute sense of hearing. The sound of Sanvi's laughter intermingled with that of Karan's from the living room was numbing my senses. I shouldn't be feeling like this. I needed this job. It was a matter of survival for me. Love decided destinies only in fairy tales. And mine couldn't be even considered as love.

It was just a crush. A one-sided affair. Crushes were only meant to give one a temporary high. I had to crush it before the bud morphed into a carnivorous flower that could consume me wholly. I was old enough to be pragmatic. All I could do was adore him from far and ensure that my obsession remained ephemeral.

Shaking my head, I picked up the headphones from the table and inserted them into my ears. Old Hindi movie songs began playing replacing the sounds drifting in from the living room. My racing heart slowed down and my temporary blindness vanished. I began to enter the data into the spreadsheet open on the computer.

After watching Sanvi and Karan together, it had taken a lot of effort to act nonchalant in front of the members of the family and other staff. The house was buzzing about their marriage. Sanvi was a regular at the house now. I'd was also hearing a lot about her from the other staff during dinner. Sanvi was the daughter of a family friend of the Varmas' and the families were close, even though Sanvi's family had migrated to New Zealand five years ago. Sanvi visited every year. Karan and Madhumita returned her visits by visiting her family in New Zealand often.

"I never thought they'd be getting married. They look more like siblings to me. But what can we say about youngsters nowadays! They are friends one day and lovers the next. I used to love seeing their camaraderie. Now it is just another love story." The cook had lamented when one of the maids had broken the news about the rumoured marriage. Though Madhumita or Karan had not made a formal declaration yet, the news had spread among the staff like wildfire. As the saying went, maybe even walls had ears. The majority of the staff had welcomed the news. They all liked Sanvi.

"Thank God it is her. I was dreading it'd be some bitch sitting on a high horse and making our lives hell," one of the housemaids had declared.

"When is the wedding? They do make a lovely couple," Raju had asked. Though I liked Raju, I had a sudden urge to punch him for saying that.

Alright. I couldn't deny that they made a lovely couple; Sanvi was the right match for Karan. Attractive, sophisticated and rich. Not an orphan like me who lived from day to day. Not someone who didn't dare to dream.

Sanvi was certainly someone who went after her dreams and chased them till she made every single one of them come true.

For me, dreams would always remain dreams. Fate had always been cruel to me. Else, my parents wouldn't have died leaving me alone at the mercy of someone as cruel as Neeru Aunty. They had been so assured about their happiness that they hadn't considered that one day their daughter might become an orphan. It hadn't been a possibility and hence they didn't leave anything for me. To add to that, Neeru Aunty had been cunning enough to threaten and cajole Grandma into signing over all her properties to them. I had lived most of my life on my own, determined to survive, even when Lavanya and Neeru Aunty made me work like a common maid. I could survive this too.

Truth be told, it had been a foolish thing to allow the seed of love to blossom inside my heart. I should have nipped it off right when it raised its audacious head. It was still not late. I could do it. Nay. I would do it.

Work became easy when determination became my wake-up call. I finished the fifty-page long spreadsheet and emailed it to Madhumita Ma'am and Karan. Then I saved it on the company cloud account, took a printout and created a backup on a storage drive as well. Karan had instructed me to follow these steps for every important document.

Leaning back in the chair, I took off the earplugs and kept them on the table. I twirled around on the chair and faced the window that overlooked the driveway of the house. When I opened my eyes, after closing them momentarily, a familiar figure appeared in the driveway. Karan had his back toward me and was talking on the phone. He ran his fingers through his hair as he listened.

Was there some problem? I wondered if I could be of any help. If I could wipe away his troubles, I would do that without a moment's delay. Unfortunately, I would have no opportunity to do that. Except for those magical hours in his company on the night of the party, he had never been close to me. The relationship between us currently was that of a strict yet kind employer and his employee. An involuntary sigh escaped me.

"Are you done with your day's work?"

Sanvi's voice startled me and I turned to face her. "Yes. I was just about to leave."

"Awesome. I wanted to ask you something." Sanvi approached the table and sat on the chair across mine.

"Will you help me plan the wedding? The wedding date is just a month away and I don't have any family or friends to support me. I cannot burden Karan and Madhu Aunty anymore. It'd be great if you can help me choose my wedding dress and my wardrobe. Please tell me you will help me."

I twiddled my thumb as I thought. Could I trust myself to do this? Wouldn't my heart make life miserable if I spent hours helping Karan's would-be wife?

"I don't know anything about dresses. You should ask someone else," I said.

"I just want someone with me who would give me their honest opinion," said Sanvi.

I searched for more excuses. But again, my status here was that of a helper in the household. I should keep their guests happy, shouldn't I?

"If Madhumita Ma'am has no objection, I can help."

"I asked her already. Are you okay with it?"

I hesitated before nodding. Of course, I would make sure that the man I loved had a memorable day when he married his beloved.

Sanvi cheered and thanked me profusely.

"We've to leave for dress hunting early tomorrow morning. I've made appointments with a designer. I wish to try out as many dresses from their collection as possible before deciding on my dream dress."

Just then, the door to the home office opened and Karan walked in. Sanvi ran to him and held his arm.

"You know what? I got a helper. Chandni has agreed to help me find my dream wedding dress," said Sanvi.

"Didn't I say I would accompany you?" Karan asked, his arms akimbo. Was he annoyed that I was going to disrupt their pleasant togetherness? If he didn't want me to go, perhaps I shouldn't.

"I don't trust your judgment. I want to hear Chandni's opinion."

Karan sighed and turned to face me. Blood rushed into my face, my cheeks heated up and the hair on my nape stood up in attention like a bunch of loyal soldiers. Would I always have this kind of reaction when Karan looked at me? God help me.

"Chandni, you don't have to do this. It is not part of your duties," said Karan, his voice soft. My heart melted on hearing him uttering my name.

"It's okay, Sir. I am free tomorrow anyway," I managed.

"Alright. Do as you wish," said Karan and walked out of the room dragging Sanvi with him.

I stared after them as my chest grew heavy. How was I going to survive this ordeal? Was there a way out?

As I slowly entered oblivion guided by the sleep-goddess that night, I continued to fiercely hold onto the memories of that one magical night. I fell asleep, wondering how my heart had deftly eliminated the bad moments and magnified the good moments.

14

KARAN

I dragged Sanvi to the porch and then let go of her abruptly. She yelped as she regained her balanced and scowled at me.

"What are you up to? I told you to leave her alone, didn't I?"

"Relax, Karan. You will thank me later. Left alone, you both will take years to get together. She is resisting and you are allowing her," said Sanvi.

"I am going in right now and telling her the truth." I pivoted on my heels and headed toward the house.

Sanvi ran after me. "Hey, I was just trying to tease you into confessing. You go and tell her. But I do need her help. That part was genuine."

"Let me tell her the truth then. You can take her with you after that."

"I think your grand revelation will have to wait. I saw Chandni heading to her room while you were dramatically dragging me here. She must have thought you couldn't wait to get me alone." Sanvi giggled and ran away before I could react.

That girl! She was truly driving me crazy.

I rushed into the house and went in the direction of the staff quarters. My sales manager called just then and I was glued to the phone for the next fifteen minutes finalizing the details of an upcoming sales meeting.

When I finally entered the staff quarters, I found it deserted as most of the staff was still at work. All the better. But when I knocked on Chandni's door, no one answered even though I continued to knock for a while.

"Sir, what are you doing here?" It was Raju who was coming down from his room on the second floor.

"Did you see Chandni? I wanted a word with her."

"Chandni? She left for her friends' place a while ago. She said it is her friend's birthday today."

I had lost yet another chance to come clean. In the business world, a delay of a few hours could make or break a company. Wasn't that true when it came to matters of the heart too? Relationships were held together by fragile threads. If one snapped, things might never be the same again.

Should I go after Chandni now? But she had anyway promised to accompany Sanvi. I would have to accompany them. There was no other way. I didn't want to risk leaving Chandni in Sanvi's company. If she was truly in love with me, as Sanvi believed, I wanted to tell her that she was all that I wanted.

She should know that I couldn't sleep at night because my mind was busy obsessing over her. Every single moment I had spent with her would come alive and shoo away my sleep. A strange heaviness would descend on my heart making it difficult to even breathe. I'd had enough. She appeared always so near and yet so far. I wanted the distance to vanish. I wanted to breathe the same air as her every second of my life. All I wished for was for her to walk into the circle of my arms and stay there.

Many moments, when she was just a hand's length away from me, in the study or the car or whenever we met in the compound, I had a hard time admitting that she was still an employee in my household.

She hadn't permitted me to consider her as anything else.

She hadn't given me a reason to believe that her heart ached for me the way mine did for her.

She always appeared polite, nervous and uninterested. But was that just an act she was putting up? Was she really in love with me as Sanvi and Mom believed? Sanvi would not have behaved this way if she didn't think Chandni loved me.

Sanvi was experienced in matters of the heart. I should believe her. Hadn't she been in love with the same man for years?

Sanvi and Ashutosh, her would-be-husband, had been my schoolmates. I hadn't realized that they were in love until six months after they started dating while in the twelfth grade. Sanvi loved to tease me about being so obviously blind to what was happening right under my nose. But who knew that when they met for group studies at my home, a romance was brewing between them? After being in a long-distance relationship since then and still so much in love, they had now decided to tie the knot against the wishes of Sanvi's parents. Though I had tried my best to convince them, Sanvi's parents wouldn't hear a thing. They had arranged a match for Sanvi with a billionaire in their circle. Ashutosh worked as a professor in a government college in Delhi. He was not someone they had envisioned as the husband of their only daughter.

Sanvi had always dreamed of getting married in Lonavala, where Ashutosh had proposed to her during our graduation days. It had happened during one of our staff trips to Lonavala. Ashutosh and Sanvi had tagged along and it was there that they had decided to be each other's forever.

Unfortunately, the resort had been fully booked for this season and Sanvi only had a month-long vacation during which she planned to tie the knot. She had left her home in New Zealand after convincing her parents that she deserved a final vacation in India before she married the man of their choice. Her parents had reluctantly agreed after Sanvi had somehow convinced them that she had cut ties with Ashutosh, who now worked in Delhi.

Months ago, when Sanvi had talked about going against her family to be with Ashutosh, I had been against the idea. Ashutosh was a good person. But I also knew the person Sanvi's parents had chosen for her. In my eyes, they had chosen the right person for her. He could give Sanvi the kind of life she was accustomed to, whereas, with Ashutosh, she would have to adjust to an upper-middle-class lifestyle. I hadn't been able to understand why Sanvi would be ready to sacrifice her inheritance and a promising career in New Zealand all for the sake of love.

But now, I understood her recklessness and even approved of it. Wouldn't I act the same way if I was in her shoes? Wouldn't I leave everything to be with Chandni? I would gladly give up my riches if that was the way to be with her. And I had only just fallen in love. If I had been in love with her for years, the way Sanvi and Ashutosh were, there wouldn't have been any doubt in my mind at all. Now I understood the strength of love; I understood how love changed people's lives.

Just a few months ago, I would have laughed if anyone told me that I would think this way. I wasn't someone who believed in love. I had always viewed marriage as a necessary evil. I was even mentally prepared to endure it. I had seen my friends getting married and succumbing to the burden of new responsibilities. Marriage had been something I had hoped to steer clear of until I couldn't avoid it any longer. But now, making Chandni my own seemed to be the only overpowering thought every single day.

The wish of seeing her pretty face was what made me get out of bed daily. Days became brighter when I saw her smile. I wanted to be wherever she was. Her laughter could drive away any anxiety within moments.

I just wished she stopped running away from me. Why couldn't she love me back? Couldn't I make her fall in love with me?

15

CHANDNI

It took me more than ten minutes to find the boutique even after arriving at the location Sanvi had sent me. It was strategically stationed on the third floor of one of the biggest malls in the area. One of those high-end shops I would've never stepped into normally.

The first person I saw when I finally reached the boutique was Karan. He was seated inside the shop on a couch meant for visitors, looking elegant in a plain white T-shirt and khakis. How could he look so handsome even when dressed so casually?

Hesitating to enter, I stood outside watching Karan. He had his iPad in his left hand and the Apple pencil in his right. The sight made me smile. It was just like him to think about work even today, even here. As I watched, he tucked the pencil into the holder on the iPad pouch and picked up a glass of juice from the coffee table in front of him. He seemed to be studying something on his iPad as he sipped the juice. Setting the glass back, he perused, picked up the stylus again and began writing. I could gaze at him the whole day and not be tired. Chiding myself for being silly, I exhaled to regain composure. And like an unexpected storm, sadness began to gather strength inside me once again.

I slipped into the shop trying to be as inconspicuous as possible but Karan looked up from his iPad just then. He slipped the iPad into his bag, stood up and approached me with a bright smile. My heart fluttered. As usual, he smelled expensive, with his fine clothes, and a pleasant mix of cologne, soap and perhaps his aftershave.

If I wasn't aware that Karan and Sanvi were getting married, I would have tagged Karan's reaction upon seeing me into the he-is-interested-in-me category. I bit my inner cheek to curb that train of thought. Ignoring my erratically thumping heart, I smiled and greeted him.

"Good morning, Chandni. Sanvi will be late as she has gone to the airport."

"Airport? But why?"

"She has gone to pick up her fiancé."

"Fiancé? But that is..." I broke off. I swallowed staring at Karan who appeared to be trying hard not to laugh.

"I know, I know. You thought she was marrying me. Thank God that is not the case," he said, flashing a grin again.

Happiness surged through me and laughter burst out of my mouth. He was not engaged to Sanvi! What delightful news! But it didn't make sense. Karan's gaze seemed to be assessing my reaction.

It wasn't proper to appear so thrilled. I quickly cleared my throat. "I am sorry. I don't know why I came to that conclusion. Maybe because Sanvi was saying you were about to make her dreams come true the other day. And I thought..."

"Is that the sign of a true lover? Do you expect that your lover will make all your dreams come true?" teased Karan.

I didn't know how to respond and just stood staring at the carpet.

"Okay, Sanvi asked me to take good care of you till she came. How about some ice cream? I am craving some."

"Sure."

I followed him even as I secretly analysed the various facts.

Karan wasn't getting married to Sanvi.

He was still unattached.

He still thought fondly of the girl at the ball.

But did these signify that I had a chance? He still didn't know that I was the mystery girl. Maybe it was time to confess the truth. Come what may, I was going to tell him everything at the first possible chance.

At the ice cream shop, Karan sat next to me on a round table that could seat four.

"Do you have any preference?"

"I am allergic to peanuts. So, anything that doesn't have peanuts would do," I said as we were going through the list of fruit salads and ice-creams.

"Oh! Good that you told me. I'll check to ensure there aren't traces of peanuts in any of the items you order," said Karan.

I chose an ice cream sundae and Karan chose a fruit salad. As we waited for our items to arrive, I tried to talk to Karan. I stuttered and stopped multiple times. Words simply failed to materialize. The romantic songs that kept playing inside the cafe also didn't help.

"What is going on in your mind? Do you want to tell me something?" asked Karan, finally, as he studied my face intently.

A nervous tingle tore through me as I gazed into his eyes. I adjusted my spectacles and squeezed my eyes shut. My throat had gone all dry. I should just forget about it. I would never gather enough courage to tell him. And soon, someone like Sanvi would arrive and steal him from me forever. That was a paralyzing thought.

And then, I felt my chair move—Karan was pulling my chair towards his. He leaned closer when we were just inches apart, his hands still holding the chair, even as I froze in place.

"How long are you going to pretend anyway? You think I didn't recognise you?" he whispered into my ears.

Startled by his words, I moved back. But Karan caught my hand and weaved his fingers through mine. "Please, love. If you like me even a little, stop torturing me. Do you even know how much I love you?"

My jaw dropped open. Could this be real? The hairs on my nape, those loyal soldiers in my heart's army, stood up in attention. If this was a dream, I didn't want it to end. I pinched my arm and winced when I felt the pain.

Watching me, Karan chuckled.

"But when..." I asked.

"Within minutes after our eyes met. The day I gave you a lift in my car for the first time."

I gasped.

"And all these days, you pretended as if you hadn't..."

"You thought only you could play the game? You gave me such a hard time these past days."

Then he raised my hand to his lips and kissed my knuckles. I sighed softly as my heart began a victory dance and I squeezed his hand in acknowledgement.

"I am sorry. I couldn't believe a man like you could like a girl like me even though...even though I loved you right from the beginning."

"A girl like you? I fell for you at first sight! But you, you have tortured me for so long. I find it difficult even now to believe that you are here, sitting right next to me, my princess. Even though you didn't leave behind a glass slipper and I am no prince, I somehow finally found my Cinderella. I could hardly function after you left me that day at the ball. I couldn't sleep or eat properly. Not a moment passed when I didn't think of you. I had plunged myself into work to distract myself."

His lips lingered on my knuckles and grazed on them again, as pleasure and contentment surged through me.

Someone cleared their throat audibly near our table and said with a snicker, "Ugh! Find a room, guys!" Sanvi stood holding the arm of a handsome young man— her fiancé.

Karan continued to hold onto my hand even though a goofy grin had appeared on his face. He looked fondly at me and introduced Ashutosh, Sanvi's fiancé, to me. Realizing that we were at a public place and that we had an audience now, I hastily withdrew my hand. I bowed my head at Ashutosh in greeting.

Sanvi and Ashutosh sat at our table. What a lovely pair they made!

"Ashu, maybe you should learn a thing or two from Karan. See, he is treating her so well. When was the last time you treated me so nicely?" Sanvi pouted.

"Ten minutes ago? Remember what we did before we got out of the car?" Ashutosh replied and Sanvi blushed.

At that moment, I felt Karan's hand on mine again. Even though he had only touched my hand, I felt warm all over. As if he had pulled me into an embrace, my whole body tingled. My eyes darted to Karan's and the sparkle in his eyes kindled a fierce fire inside me. Intense, all-encompassing and precious.

Karan held my hand whenever he could as we walked around the mall and inside the boutique. Though I hesitated initially, I began to miss his touch acutely whenever we couldn't hold hands.

While Ashutosh was busy appreciating the various wedding gowns that Sanvi tried on, Karan grabbed a red gown and insisted on buying it for me for Sanvi's wedding. He refused to listen to any of my arguments against it.

"Wear this and let me see if this is enough. I want my girl to look the prettiest at my best friend's wedding."

I reluctantly went to the trial room to change. When I tried it on, the gown looked as if it had been created for me. It hugged my curves, the soft silk felt wonderful against my skin and made me look elegant.

When I stepped out of the dressing room, I wondered if Karan would like it.

"How is it?" I asked, standing on the small podium in the VIP area. Karan, who was seated on the couch inside the room, glanced up.

Without a word, he stood up, strolled towards me with a frown on his face and paused at a hand's length from me. Then lowering his voice, he said, "It is perfect. But it tempts me to go on an exploration." Even as I pondered as to what he meant, he traced one finger lightly up my left arm, its traitorous journey leaving goosebumps behind. I grabbed his finger when it skipped over the sleeves and landed on my shoulders.

"Karan?" I murmured.

"Yes?"

"Stop messing with me."

"God knows who is messing with whom," he whispered, a smile playing on his lips. He dropped a quick kiss on my cheeks before returning to his seat.

All I could do then was stare at him as heat began to pool in my belly.

When we returned to the Varma Mansion, my heart was overflowing with the happy memories we had created that day. My hands were full of gifts Karan had lavished on me.

How had I turned so lucky?

Maybe that is why they called this experience falling in love. When we fell in love, we fell blindly, confident that our lovers will pick us up. That they would carry us in their arms and keep us secure, safe and warm on any stormy day.

It was as if my fairy Godmother had waved her magic wand and sprinkled fairy dust on me. Suddenly, my life was filled with rainbows, music and a love that made everything sparkle.

16

KARAN

Unlike usual, Chandni had thrown open her window and was watching as I swam in the pool. With her elbows propped up on the window sill and her palms cupping her face, she resembled a happy child. I sent a flying kiss her way. She smiled making my lips turn upwards. I signalled to her, asking if I could go to her, and climbed out of the pool. She shook her head but I was not ready to accept that. Tilting my head to the side, I put my palms together and mouthed, "Please." She shook her head again.

As I dried myself with a towel, I glanced at her window. She was gone. Determined to have my way, I headed to her room and knocked. Chandni opened her door but stood at the door with her eyes wide with surprise. I loved how her eyes stealthily inspected my upper body. I had pulled on my pyjamas over the swimming tights but had only my bath towel to cover my torso.

"What are you doing? What will the others think?"

"They will think I am your lover, which, of course, is the truth," I said as I entered her room. Her room was just like her. Simple and filled with grace. Her course books occupied a tiny shelf, the bed was neatly made and not a single item seemed out of place or dirty. A tiny Ganesha idol made of silver basked in the light of the brass oil lamp lit in front of it. An incense was infusing the fragrance of sandalwood into the room.

"Oof! I don't want them to misunderstand me. Please go, Karan."

I didn't budge from my spot even as Chandni gave me a slight push. Involuntarily my eyes roved over her. She was dressed in a white cotton churidar. Her hair was still wet from the shower and, as usual, there wasn't a trace of makeup on her face. Yet, it glowed with a healthy sheen making my heart thrum. Her rosy lips lured me and I was so ready to give in to temptation.

"I will go if you return what I gave you earlier."

"What did you give me?"

"A kiss."

Chandni was taken aback. "But when?"

"At the pool. Just minutes ago. How could you forget?" I pouted.

Chandni smiled and sent a flying kiss in my direction.

"Not enough."

"Karan."

"At least give me one here," I said, tapping my right cheek with my index finger.

After hesitating for a moment, Chandni came closer, stood on her toes and pressed her lips on my cheek. God help me, the temptation just grew manifold. Chandni moved away. "Now go."

"Now, this is a total imbalance. Give one on my other cheek too, it is complaining."

"Grow up, Karan. Go now."

"I won't until I get what is due."

"Oof! Fine."

Chandni came closer and stood on her toes again. Just as her lips were nearing my cheek, I turned my face making her lips land on mine. The feather touch sent a bolt of electricity straight down my spine. With a groan, I cupped her cheeks and claimed what I had wanted all along. I kissed her the way I had dreamed about. Pulling her against me, I pressed my mouth to hers, demanding, possessing and owning her. I ran my tongue along her open lips and teased her until she moaned. My heart was thumping wildly and I was getting aroused with each touch and stroke. I stopped before the urge to drag her to bed like a man bewitched by lust overpowered me. Looking deeply into her eyes, I tenderly kissed her cheeks one after the other.

"Become mine soon. Or I will go crazy," I whispered, and then reluctantly took a step away from her. I touched her arm lightly before turning away. When I was at her door, I remembered what I had forgotten to say.

"From today, I want us to have breakfast together. Mom must have already informed the staff about us. So, don't fret over it. Also, she wants to talk to you about something important. Be there in half an hour. Okay, love?"

Chandni appeared dazed. Her lips were red and swollen from my kisses but her eyes sparkled. She looked a hundred times more enticing. Dear God! I needed another plunge in the pool.

Last night, Mom had been thrilled when I had told her that I was in love with Chandni and that she loved me too.

"I am so happy for you, son. I am grateful you found true love." Those had been her exact words. She had immediately begun to pester me about setting a wedding date.

"She doesn't have any relatives other than those wretched Malhotras. We cannot make her stay at the staff quarters any longer."

"She can move into my room any time, you know," I teased her.

"Only after you take the wedding vows with her. Marriage is not a joke. I want you to have a long and happy life with her. You can get engaged as soon as I get a date from our astrologer."

I was only too eager to comply. I wanted Chandni in my life as soon as possible.

Breakfast was a happy affair that morning. I cheerfully nodded to everything that Mom said as she was speaking and behaving exactly as I wanted. Mom and Chandni had already bonded well over the past month and the new developments had made Mom don the role of a loving mother instead of that of her employer.

"We will have a private engagement ceremony this weekend with a few friends and family. I don't think I have to seek permission from the Malhotras even though they are your only relatives. Not after they threw you out of the house unceremoniously," said Madhumita.

"Yes. I agree," I said.

"Did I ask you?" Mom turned to me and cocked an eyebrow.

Chandni paused eating upon hearing Mom's statement. After remaining silent for a few minutes, she spoke, "They won't be interested in what is happening to me. They will be glad that they don't have to be bothered about me anymore. Grandma was my only other living relative I know of. After she passed away, I was dreading the day when I would be thrown out of that house. My parents died in a fire incident while we were vacationing in Bali. If I hadn't wandered out with a friend I had made there, I would have died with them."

Mom looked at Chandni and she looked at me as if she had just realized something. "Karan, do remember that friend you made in Bali years ago? That little girl who cried all night in my arms after she lost her parents in a fire."

Chandni was that girl? The memory of that night, when flares had swallowed that little vacation bungalow in Bali, still evoked terror inside me. I remember hugging her tight to prevent her from running into the burning building as she called out to her parents. I had been terrified of fire for a long time afterwards and my parents had taken me to a counsellor to help me get over the trauma. When I looked at Chandni then, the face of my little friend became clearer again.

I was ten then. Chandni must have been four or five years old. For a full week, she had been my playmate in that quaint little resort. Our parents had bonded as well. At that time, we were living in London and had been in Bali for a two-week-long vacation. We returned to India and settled in Mumbai only five years after that painful incident.

"Wait. Give me a moment," said Mom as she went to her room.

"So, how many times are you going to save me, Karan?" Chandni asked, her eyes welling with tears.

Pulling her into an embrace, I smoothed her hair and placed a kiss on her forehead. I didn't know what to say. Were our destinies so closely intertwined? But I wished our shared memory from childhood was less traumatic. Chandni snuggled closer to me and I knew she was struggling with the onslaught of painful memories.

"I found it. See, you used to hug her exactly this way even back then," Mom commented when she returned with an album I hadn't seen in a while. In the photo that she passed to us, I was beaming at the camera, holding Chandni within the circle of my arms.

Mom found a few other photos taken during that vacation. Chandni's eyes sparkled when she found pictures of her parents among them.

"Can I have a copy of these photos? I don't have a single photo of them with me."

"Of course. Karan make copies and get them framed for her," Mom said.

As we continued to reminisce about those days, I contemplated the life Chandni had been forced to lead.

My blood had boiled when I'd heard how the Malhotras had thrown Chandni out of their house the day after the party. Since then, I had secretly started buying shares in bulk from Malhotra Textiles in Chandni's name. As of now, I had acquired more than fifty per cent of the total shares. If rumours were to be believed, Chandni should be the rightful owner of the Malhotra Group as it was founded by her father.

Most of the major shareholders had been eager to sell because of the crises the group was going through. And while I was in talks with them, I had heard disturbing stories. How Chandni's father had signed a power of attorney to his cousin before he had left on a long-awaited vacation with his family and never returned. It had raised many eyebrows then as the incident was quickly labelled as a suicide. I wanted to get to the bottom of it all for Chandni's sake. Now I was doubly sure that it wasn't a suicide. The photos we had in our album and the memories we had told an entirely different story.

But that was all for later. Of prime importance now was to make Chandni my own as soon as possible.

Just then, my phone rang. The news that would have been welcome on any other occasion felt strangely like a sore thumb. I would be away from home for a full week starting Sunday. Right after my engagement. All my plans of spending time with Chandni were going to go for a toss.

Unless! The idea that came made me smile. I would have to use all my persuasion skills this time. I had to convince two women after all.

"Amsterdam?"

"Yes."

"You are crazy! I can't make the trip. I have other things scheduled," said Mom.

"Please, Mom. You should."

Mom narrowed her eyes as she gazed at me and then shook her head.

I spent the best of the next hour trying to convince Mom that I needed her presence on this trip to Amsterdam. And of course, Chandni needed to accompany us.

17

The sky of Lonavala was a lovely play of colours beyond the rolling blue hills of the Western Ghats on the horizon as the sun slowly bid adieu. The pleasant evening breeze played with my hair as I stood at the window watching the event planners rush around, giving final touches to the beautifully decorated terrace. Rose garlands in pink and red interspersed with dark evergreen leaves covered the pillars and the dome of the circular mandap set up for the engagement ceremony. Today, I was getting engaged to the man of my dreams.

Never in my recent life had I experienced something like the week that had passed. Every single second that ticked past touched me deeply. There had, of course, been moments of fear and uncertainties. But happiness, love and hope had arrived as a team and washed away my anxieties because of Karan and Madhumita Ma'am.

Even though they were surprised at first, the other staff at Varma Mansion had congratulated me heartily when Madhumita ma'am, Mom as she insisted I address her, announced it the Saturday before the engagement. I had been asked to shift to the main house and given the room next to my employer. Some told me I deserved him while some others said I was lucky to have Karan as a husband.

I don't know if I deserved him, but I was sure that my luck had turned. The Goddess of Luck had, for some reason, decided to be benevolent toward me all in a single week.

First, Karan had confessed his love and then showered me with love whenever he was around. Kisses and hugs from him were no longer something I yearned for, but my everyday reality. Even then, a childlike giddiness conquered me whenever he came near. We had discovered the bliss of simply smiling at each other and basking in its enchantment; we did that a lot these days.

Secondly, Karan's mom had decided it was time for us to get engaged.

It was as if miracles had become commonplace in my life. I was truly grateful for Karan's mom. If not for her, Karan wouldn't have perhaps returned to my life. Karan had told me how she had hired me as her assistant with the sole aim of putting me in his path again. Though Karan insisted that he was planning to go in search of me after he took care of some urgent work commitments, I doubted if that would have happened any time soon, given how busy Karan usually was. With time, he might have forgotten about the girl he had briefly met at the ball.

Madhumita Ma'am had easily slipped into the role of being a mother to me. She pampered me and took me out when Karan was not around. She made sure every one of her acquaintances treated me well during social outings. At a lunch meeting we attended, a meanie, who had hoped of getting her daughter married to Karan, had suddenly started slandering me.

"How can you trust such girls, Madhu? It is as clear as this water even for me. She is a gold-digger who has expertly trapped your son." The woman had whisper-shouted her advice to Madhumita Ma'am. I had winced hearing it.

Karan's mom had shaken her head in exasperation and said, "You are vainly trying to project your ideas on me. I don't doubt Chandni's sincerity or her love. It is plain meanness to talk in such a way about a person. I will let this slide this time. Don't expect me to be as forgiving the next time. I will sue you if you insult her again."

Tears had pricked the back of my eyes then. No one had ever defended me thus. I had always been at the receiving end of insults. Maybe, I had done something good in the past to have ended up having Madhumita Ma'am and Karan in my life.

Two days ago, Sanvi got married to Ashutosh here at this same venue. They were flying out to Mauritius the day after our engagement. Sanvi had become close to me during the many pre-wedding rituals and also because Sanvi's parents had disowned Sanvi after they came to know of Sanvi's decision to marry Ashutosh. They had refused to be a part of the ceremony. Karan and I had tried our best to keep Sanvi cheerful. While I made sure there weren't any glitches during the many rituals, Karan had ensured the venue looked heavenly.

"I wish I could get married like this. Without any crowd. Just an intimate, beautiful and private function with friends and family," I told Karan, as Sanvi took the *saat pheras* or the seven rounds around the holy fire during the wedding ceremony. The wedding guests mainly consisted of Ashutosh's relatives and some close friends of the bride and the groom.

"Just don't say that to Mom. She might eat you alive. She has been planning my wedding ever since I was in diapers. I used to piss her off by declaring I would never get married. But given a choice, I would prefer something like this too." Karan had said, his eyes lighting up with a mixture of mischief and love.

Sanvi came into my room just then and shouted, "So, isn't the bride-to-be ready yet?"

"I am," I said.

"You look so lovely! How did that idiot get so lucky?!" asked Sanvi, rolling her eyes. "Wait, your *maang tikka* is slightly off to the right. Let me correct it." She adjusted the said hair ornament.

Just after that, she found that a tiny decorative bead had got loose and was slightly dangling on my blouse. Making me face her, Sanvi began to inspect my makeup and hairdo.

"Oh my God! That idiot beautician has used the wrong eye shadow. I was gone only for an hour. I should just kill her."

"Hey, it is okay. Nobody would even notice," I said, knowing how easily things could get out of hand if I allowed Sanvi to run with it. Hadn't she made the beautician redraw her winged eyeliner six times in a row on the day of her wedding? I wasn't a perfectionist like her and couldn't care less about the hue of an eye shadow.

Sanvi wasn't in the mood to give up though.

"I am sleep deprived and cranky. I had to take a quick nap. That doesn't mean that she can get away with sloppy work. I am going to kill her. And then, I am going to kill my beast of a husband who kept me up all night yesterday even though he knew I was in charge today." She muttered as she stomped out of the hotel room in search of the errant beautician.

I chuckled. *Kill Ashutosh?* As if! Sanvi was equal parts of trouble and cuteness. Ashutosh doted on her. They could hardly keep their hands off each other when they were together.

Karan's mom entered the room along with Vani and Shweta who had arrived just on time. I had been worried they might not come. They had been initially furious that I had hidden such a huge secret from them. But being my true friends, they understood me when I laid out the reasons behind my lies. Other than them, I had no one to call my own. Karan's mom left the room and allowed us to catch up. Soon, it was time for the engagement.

On the stage, Karan's mom wrapped an ornate chunni around me, a family heirloom.

When the priest declared it was time for the ring ceremony, Karan dropped onto one knee in front of the couch where we were seated. Then, as everyone cheered him on, he slipped the ring on my left ring finger. I blushed furiously as happiness surged through me.

Then, placing a kiss on my hand, he made me stand next to him. He gestured for the microphone and once he got hold of the mic, he slipped his left arm around me, pulled me close and spoke,

"Remember tonight.
For it is the beginning of always.
For tonight is mere formality.
Only an announcement to the world of the feelings long held.
Promises made long ago.
In the sacred spaces of our hearts."

I smiled as the guests applauded hearing the famous quote. Shweta whistled thrice.

A lone, happy tear slipped out of my eyes as I gazed at Karan's face. My man knew exactly how to romance me. I loved that he had used Dante Alighieri's quote to seal his promise of love. It was the opening quote in my longhand journal that contained all my favourite quotes and poems. I

had caught Karan reading it a few days ago.
He was a sly thief, but definitely a keeper.

18

KARAN

Mom hadn't stopped complaining even after we arrived at the airport. If she was hoping to talk me out of this, she was doomed to fail. I was looking forward to all the things I had planned minus more interference on her part. Her presence on the trip was merely for Chandni's sake. And I had an inkling that she was aware of it. She was nagging to merely irritate me.

"You know this is going to make all my plans go haywire. Do you have any idea how much planning has to be done to pull off a proper wedding these days?"

I didn't say a word as she continued to rant about the many things she needed to take care of.

"The wedding planner was supposed to visit me this week. If you go on like this, you will have a colourless wedding."

"You know very well that I care nothing about all the frivolous activities and expenditure you are planning for the wedding, right?"

"Frivolous?! Did you just say frivolous? Do you even care that this is one of my fondest dreams? You will understand that only when you become a parent. Why am I even wasting my time talking to you? Come here, Chandni, let us look for some books to read during the trip."

Chandni gave me a cute little smile and her brown eyes pierced straight into my heart before she hurried away with mother.

I took a few deep breaths and exhaled slowly when we finally settled into our business class seats on the flight, and I felt a familiar sense of calm. It was often during long flights that I felt the calmest. When I was a child, I used to be petrified of flying. It took me a long time to get over the fear, to realize that floating thousands of feet above ground level could feel joyful. Once I'd learnt to trust its beauty, travelling in aeroplanes had become blissful.

I had booked a couple-seat for Chandni and me, which meant we occupied the adjacent seats in the middle that were slightly angled toward one another. Mom, who preferred window seats, was happy with hers even though she raised a curious brow when she saw our seats—I swear she rolled her eyes when she walked to her seat. Gosh, it was embarrassing!

"Will you hold my hands during take-off? I guess I am a bit nervous during take-offs," said Chandni softly. Her fingers were trembling slightly.

I took her hand into mine and lightly squeezed it. At that moment, when she sat beside me looking into my eyes, trusting me, I fell in love with her all over again. She made me feel like I was in her safe place. I smiled reassuringly at her to remind her that she wasn't alone. I was there, right beside her.

"There used to be a kid who was terrified of travelling in aeroplanes. All he could think of when someone mentioned aeroplanes were planes crash landing, exploding in mid-air and crashing into buildings. But he also wanted to visit and explore places, especially the exotic ones. And his dreams to visit all those exotic places could come true only if he fought and won over his fear of flying. And that was exactly what he did. The fears we avoid facing often define our limits. It took a lot of effort, breathing into paper bags and breaking out in cold sweats. But he persisted and soon, air travel became his greatest joy. Do I have to clarify that I was that boy?"

"Really? So, there is hope for me?"

"Of course," I said, "Now, tell me what it is about tulips that you love. Tomorrow, we will visit the tulip gardens at Keukenhof."

"Wow! I can't wait! Honestly, I don't know why I love tulips. I haven't even seen them other than in photos. But do you know that tulips, in the language of flowers, mean a declaration of love?"

"Is it? I had no idea."

"I first heard about it in a novel called the 'Language of Flowers' by Vanesa Diffenbaugh. Every tulip stands for a specific message based on its colour."

"Interesting."

"Wait, I have it all written down in my journal," she said. She took out her journal where she loved to jot down quotes and poems.

"Yes, here it is. The yellow tulips represent cheerful thoughts and say 'there is sunshine in your smile.' The red ones are associated with true or perfect love and say 'believe me'. Pink ones represent affection and caring and say 'I care for you'. Cream ones say 'I will love you forever'. Purple symbolizes royalty and wealth. Orange tulips symbolize energy, enthusiasm, desire and passion. Variegated tulips say 'You have beautiful eyes.' White symbolizes purity, heaven and newness. Isn't that interesting?"

"Yes. Very. I have decided to gift you tulips in all of these colours. Because you see, there is a burst of sunshine in your smile. Believe me! I do care for you. I will love you forever. For me, you represent royalty, wealth, energy, enthusiasm, desire and passion. You have beautiful eyes. For me you are everything pure and heavenly," I said, taking her journal in my hand and quoting from it.

Chandni giggled.

"If you want to hear a story about the origin of tulips, I have it too," she said.

"I would love to hear it," I said. I could listen to her for hours even if she was just reading aloud the telephone directory.

"Okay! There is this Turkish legend that talks about the love story of a prince named Farhad. He loved a beautiful maiden called Shirin. Their love was not to be and Shirin was killed by those who opposed the match. Prince Farhad, crushed by grief, killed himself by riding over the edge of a cliff. The legend goes that red tulips bloomed in places where his blood fell. Thus, red tulips came to symbolize perfect love."

"Ah, sad! Love stories shouldn't have a sad ending. There is nothing more heartbreaking than a love story that ends in a tragedy."

"You think so too? I avoid reading love stories that supposedly have a sad ending."

"Yes. That's exactly why I don't like Romeo and Juliet. Agreed they loved each other sincerely. But in my opinion, love is all about hope. If a love story doesn't teach you to believe in hope, it doesn't convey the right message, right?"

"I agree," she said beaming at me.

"And just like that, we have taken off. The flight is now up in the clouds and stable. Are you okay now?"

"I didn't even realize," she said, the smile brightening her face even more.

"Let's watch a movie," I suggested.

"Yes."

We watched the same movies back to back on our respective screens, pausing in between to share anecdotes or jokes. The only thing that made it different from a movie date was perhaps the absence of a bucket of popcorn and stolen kisses in the darkness.

We had a terminal change and a layover in Paris for over five hours. While Mom relaxed in the lounge with a new thriller she had picked up, we walked around drinking coffee and sampling sandwiches and many colourful macaroons. We also checked out the many artworks that were on loan to the airport from The Louvre, Palace of Versailles, and other institutions.

"Do you think a honeymoon in Paris could be just our thing?" I asked while we roamed around looking at artwork displaying French art and culture.

"It could be," said Chandni with a dreamy look in her eyes.

I wrapped my arms around her and tucked her into my side. I couldn't wait for those days to arrive. I saw the same eagerness in her eyes. She smiled and I pulled her closer. The source of a smile was often joy, but sometimes the source could also be a person. Just a glimpse of that individual and one's lips would automatically curl upwards in joy.

19

CHANDNI

"So, let me try to understand this—I really can't get my head around this. Your meetings have been rescheduled for next week? You plan to go sightseeing until then?" Karan's mom seemed to have lost it. She was still in her pyjamas and was sitting cross-legged on her bed. Her laptop lay open on her lap and she was glaring at Karan, her reading glasses perched low on her nose. We, Karan and I, were dressed and ready to leave for Keukenhof.

"Mom, I said my first set of meetings is scheduled for Monday. Today is Wednesday already. Our clients are busy this week, so we rescheduled them," said Karan.

Liar. I had overheard him ask his manager to reschedule them because he was busy this week. Busy because he wanted to spend this week with me. He looked so cute even when he was lying. He explained that he wanted to fulfil my dream of visiting the Keukenhof gardens before he got his head all hot after his many business meetings.

"Why am I hearing about this only now? I am not in the mood for any sightseeing now. All I can think about are guest lists, menus and hotel bookings. I can't believe this!"

"Mom, you can do it all via video conferencing and phone calls."

"Still, I don't have the energy to walk around in tulip gardens or whatever."

"Mom, it is Chandni's dream to visit the gardens. You will break her heart if you refuse."

"I refuse to come. Period. I am happy here. Here, I have a proper WiFi connection, clean rooms and Indian food. You both can go. Leave me here in peace."

Karan's face lit up as he turned to look at me. It seems he was getting exactly what he wanted. By bringing his mother, he had effectively shut the mouth of any gossiping relatives and socialites. Perhaps Karan's mom understood this and was putting up this act to give us some privacy. We had never really spent quality time with each other after our engagement as it was.

"Be back by Sunday. And keep me in the loop," said Karan's mom as she waved us out of the room.

"Sure," said Karan, walking towards me. His hand landed possessively on my waist and he grinned at me.

"And be responsible. Do you understand what I mean?" said Karan's mom.

"Yes," said Karan. His ears had turned red. I had noticed that happened whenever he was stressed or embarrassed. He was embarrassed probably. Cute!

When we settled into the car Karan had hired, his ears were still red and he was refusing to meet my eyes. I couldn't help but smile. Once I'd buckled my seatbelt, I leaned and touched his ear.

"Tell me, why are they so red..."

"Do you *really* want to hear why?" he said, emphasizing the 'really.'

I nodded.

"Did you understand what she meant by 'being responsible'?" Karan asked, a mischievous smile on his lips.

"Of course. That's what every parent tells their kid when they are going on a trip. We must be careful and be responsible. Are you embarrassed that your mother treated you like a kid in front of me?"

"You are so naive! Love, we are an unwed couple going on a trip to a romantic location. What might she have meant by asking us to be responsible?"

A wholly different sort of explanation unceremoniously popped into my mind. It was my turn to be embarrassed. Did she really mean that? I heard Karan chuckle.

"Boy oh boy! You surely have a gutter mind. I didn't mean any of what you just thought. I was talking about being responsible while driving, obeying traffic rules etc."

"I *was* thinking about those things too," I said, looking away and fanning my face to cool down my cheeks that were burning like hot coals.

"Oh, so thinking about a long drive makes you all hot and bothered?" he asked, that teasing smile making an appearance again.

"Karan! Stop messing with my head."

"I did nothing of the sort. Blame it on all those romances that you keep reading. Long drives equal handholding, stolen kisses, overnight stay means sleeping together..."

"Ugh, you are the worst tease in the world." Gosh! Those were the very thoughts that had crossed my mind. Was he clairvoyant or something? But whatever! It was too embarrassing to know that he saw through me so easily.

"Am I now?" Karan asked, raising a questioning brow at me.

I remained silent as he reversed the car and got onto the highway. Five minutes into the drive, he patted my arm lightly. He found my hand and squeezed it lightly.

"Sorry. Don't be upset. I was only teasing. My ears turned red because I had been thinking about those very things."

I narrowed my eyes at him.

"Now who has the gutter mind here? A man and a woman can travel together and be responsible. I believe that," I said, trying hard not to laugh. Karan chuckled and I burst out laughing.

I liked how he always made me laugh. I liked his jokes. And I loved the many rituals he had created for us. Every day, he made sure to call and talk to me on the phone the moment he was free, even if he was busy with countless meetings for the rest of the day. He never forgot to smuggle in a warm hug before we bid each other good night.

Another thing that made it easier to bond with him was that he was a good listener. I could talk to him about anything in the world. If anything made me feel sad or awkward, he would immediately crack a joke, dissolving any tension that might have built up within me. I loved him so much that I feared hurting him even with a wayward word. He was that precious to me.

Keukenhof Gardens was 40 KM away from Amsterdam and it took about 40 minutes for us to reach there. As we drove past, the countryside of Bollenstreek charmed us with its fantastical rainbow-hued scenery. I felt as if we were entering paradise. My heart sang.

Located in the town of Lisse, the Keukenhof gardens, with over 7 million flowers blooming each year, were one of the largest flower gardens in the world. The fragrance of spring flowers greeted us as we entered the garden. Neat rows of hyacinths, daffodils, orchids, lilies, roses, irises, tulips and other spring flowers vied for our attention. Wherever we turned, colours greeted us. Many pavilions offered to teach us gardening skills, and landscaping ideas and also had mouth-watering food.

At a pavilion where we could learn about the history of the gardens, we learned that the grounds of Keukenhof were part of Countess Jacqueline of Bavaria's estate. In Dutch, Keukenhof meant kitchen garden. Originally, these gardens supplied the herbs used in the kitchen in the castle of Jacqueline, the countess of Teylingen. In 1950, the garden was thrown open to the public, thus turning Keukenhof into a spring park.

The Keukenhof castle was nearby and we mentally made a note to visit it once we finished touring the garden which was 36 hectares. It would surely take days if we were to enjoy it to the fullest and visit every corner of the garden.

Another interesting feature was that every year the garden followed a theme. The theme this year was 'Romance in Flowers'. A couple of inspirational gardens in the same style as the theme were created to be used as an inspiration to style personal gardens or balconies. There were many new gardens introduced this year to match the theme—like the Cupid's Garden, the holiday romance garden, the hipster garden and many more.

In Cupid's Garden, there was a kissing gate that was surrounded by red and white flowers. Karan was quite delighted by the theme and kissed me amid the blooming flowers. Thank God we were not alone. Almost all the couples inside the area were using Cupid as a reason to kiss.

"Look there. Can you see that flowering tree next to the fountain?"

"Yes."

"A few years ago, beneath that cherry blossom tree, two star-crossed lovers from London committed suicide by consuming poison. It is said that the ghosts of the couple wander these gardens and sometimes enter into conversations with strangers. The strangest thing is that all the couples who talk to them break up immediately after leaving the garden. It is a sort of a dreaded legend around here," said Karan as we were walking toward the fountain.

Involuntarily, my hand tightened around his. I looked around looking for possible contenders for the doomed ghost couple. A young couple sitting beneath the cherry blossom tree was waving at us. The young man got up and took a step toward us.

"Let's move away from here, please." My heart began to race as I watched the young man approaching us. His feet were definitely on the ground. If he was a ghost, he would have floated towards us. Not walked. Still, I clutched at Karan's hand and turned to him.

Karan puffed his cheeks and laughed out loud when his eyes met mine.

"You are such an innocent. I made up that story just now."

I punched him squarely on his ribs.

"Ahhh, that hurt! That *really* hurt," he cried.

"You had it coming," I said.

"Can you click a pic for us, please," asked the young man who had by now reached near us.

As it turned out, the young couple were indeed from London. Karan smirked at me once they introduced themselves. I rolled my eyes. Karan talked with them for a while and then we bid goodbye to them and parted ways.

"I didn't know I could make up such accurate stories. They are already married though."

"Oh, so they had a bottle of poison inside their backpack as well? Maybe we should report before they turn into ghosts," I teased.

As we progressed through the garden, Karan kept me entertained similarly. It was fun to play along, hearing him create stories about the origin of many inanimate objects that we found along the way. Time flew and our bond grew stronger. We walked while sharing secrets, fears and personal anecdotes that at times brought tears of joy into my eyes.

Our plan to visit the Keukenhof castle was shelved as we were informed that the attic of the castle was undergoing renovation. Visitors were not allowed until the renovations were completed.

So, we decided to visit the vast tulip gardens where we hoped to wander among endless fields of tulips. We hired an eco-friendly electric car provided by a company that provided GPS-based tours with audio guides within the tulip fields in the area around Keukenhof.

Once there, the Bollywood aficionados inside us raised their goofy heads. Karan ran ahead after thrusting the camera at me.

"Record a video first and then click pics, okay?" Karan shouted and then struck the open arms signature pose of Shahrukh Khan.

I watched him fondly as he maintained the pose for my benefit. At that moment, all images of Shahrukh striking the pose faded and were quickly replaced by that of Karan.

"Good that you listened to me and wore this plain yellow chiffon sari. You will look like Sridevi if you run through these fields. I am reminded of the movie Chandni," said Karan.

"No. If you are Shahrukh, I am Kajol," I said. There wasn't a better-matched couple than Shahrukh-Kajol.

"Okay, my Kajol! Your wish is my command," said Karan.

A lot more photos and a million memories later, when we finally reached our vacation rental, the sun was already setting. The sight of the place we were staying made my jaws drop.

This was to be our home for the next three days? The waterfront holiday home on the island, De Kaag, Karan had booked was a three-bedroom luxury villa!

"Isn't this a bit too much for just the two of us? We could have stayed at a hotel instead," I asked, hesitating at the front door.

"I didn't want to cancel just because Mom chose not to come. But I am sure you will not regret the stay here," Karan said, letting me into the house.

On the ground floor, there was a double bedroom with an en-suite bathroom. The bed especially looked inviting after the long hours we had spent roaming around. But when I saw the upstairs bedroom with a balcony that had a lake view, I immediately sat on that bed and smiled at Karan.

"Mr Karan Varma. This is mine," I said.

"I am sorry, but I will be sleeping here today," he said.

"Are you seriously going to fight with me over this?" I asked, raising my brows.

"Maybe not. But we can share it, you know?" Karan asked hopefully.

"Remember what your Mom said? Be a responsible adult. Out. Now," I said playfully pushing him out of the room. Karan pouted. I shut the door as he began to protest. After a while, I heard him walk down the stairs. As I lay back on the bed, I suddenly felt lonely for the first time in the day.

After taking a shower, I changed into a comfortable dress and headed downstairs. The bedroom door downstairs was closed and I could hear slow music coming from the inside. The living room with the open kitchen was equipped with all modern amenities. The fridge was well stocked. There were bowls of fruits on the island that separated the kitchen from the living room. I found various kinds of bread, cereals and spices in the storage cabinets.

And that gave me an idea. I checked the fridge and the spice cabinet. Yes, I had all the necessary ingredients.

20

KARAN

I had dreamed about something like this multiple times. Walking in on my woman cooking for me. At home, I had never seen her cook, though I had eaten some of the dishes she had cooked for me with the cook's permission.

Pausing in the living room, I gazed at her. My heart fluttered as I took in her lovely form. The visual was so much better than my imagination. Dressed in a pink floral dress, she looked delectable from every angle. Her hair was scooped up using a scrunchie. A few strands had escaped from the messy knot and were fluttering and curling around her lovely neck. Was it the scent of whatever she had cooked that made my mouth water or was it the sight of her?

I noticed that she had switched back to wearing her glasses though she'd been wearing her contacts all day. I was confused as to which look I preferred more. My only complaint was that her glasses hid the attractiveness of her evocative eyes.

With my eyes focused on her, I tiptoed toward her intending to catch her by surprise. Just then, my foot got hooked on the living room rug and I stumbled and fell overturning a flower vase on the side table.

Chandni turned hearing the ruckus. "Are you okay?" She ran to me.

"I am," I said sheepishly, dusting myself off as I stood up.

"Dinner is almost ready. Give me ten more minutes," she said, smiling at me.

"But why are you doing this? You must be tired after roaming all day. I was planning to order in," I confessed.

"I love cooking. It is a quick dinner. Nothing elaborate. I have made your favourite egg fried rice along with some braised chicken." She went back to cutting cucumbers and carrots for the salad.

Picking up a piece of carrot from the cutting board, I tossed it into my mouth. Stepping around her, I pressed my lips on her nape and embraced her from behind. She smelled of *parijats*. A sigh of pleasure escaped from her lips and I pressed another kiss below her ears. She trembled.

"Karan, please don't. Let me finish this."

"Mmm. Stay still. I love your fragrance. If not for this, I might be still searching for you."

"Then you should be thanking my Grandma for teaching me how to make a cosmetic cream using them."

"You make it? The smell is so easy on the nose and kind of enchanting. Maybe you should start manufacturing it commercially. Yes, I will create a manufacturing unit for you. I am sure it is going to dance off our shelves within no time."

"You are giving wings to my dreams! But is that possible?"

Chandni freed herself from my arms and transferred the veggies to a serving bowl. Then she walked to the dining table and placed the bowl at its centre.

"Why not? The Varma group has already entered the cosmetic industry and our products are huge hits already.

I am sure this cream will take us to a whole new level. Especially as it is completely organic."

I took the plates, glasses and cutlery she had washed, dried them with a cloth towel, and placed them on the table.

"Sounds great. Maybe one day I can do that," Chandni said as she brought the braised chicken and egg fried rice to the table.

"Wow, this looks yummy. Wait, a bit more aesthetic needed."

I had seen two beautifully shaped, huge scented candles in the living room cabinet earlier. I placed them at the centre of the table, lit them and then switched off the lights in the dining room.

"Perfect. Time for a romantic, candlelit dinner with my sweetheart."

I was already head over heels in love with the woman who sat before me, but the taste of the food she had cooked made my adoration soar higher. God had truly given me a treasure.

When we were almost done with dinner, I insisted on washing the dishes. She agreed. Chandni took the washed dishes and dried them. After instructing me to place the plates, glasses and cutlery back where they belonged, Chandni walked away saying she'd just remembered something. She arrived a few minutes later armed with two bowls full of chocolate ice cream. Sitting on the kitchen counter, she scooped a spoonful into her mouth.

"Ah, it is so yum, try it," she said and our eyes locked. My gaze dropped to her lips. The sight of chocolate smeared on her lips made me drool.

I strode to her, cupped her face in my hands, traced her lips with my tongue and licked off the ice cream from her lips.

"Yes. I agree."

Chandni pushed me off with a giggle.

"That seemed straight out of the romance I read yesterday. You stole it from there, didn't you?"

"What? You wound me. That was impulsive," I complained.

Her dark eyes narrowed. "As if," she muttered.

"Good that you reminded me of that book, though. I did see glimpses of what you were reading. And although what I did just now was completely my idea, I clearly remember reading about the hero using the kitchen counter in a memorable way."

Chandni gasped and her skin flushed. God, I loved teasing her. It was my turn to laugh as she jumped off the countertop.

I leaned on the counter and scooped a spoonful and gazed at Chandni hungrily as the ice cream slowly melted in my mouth. She avoided meeting my eyes and continued eating her ice cream silently. I hadn't ever thought that merely glancing at her eating dessert would wind me up like this. Each lick and slurp made my heart pound. My eyes seemed obsessed with her lips and it was as if everything except her lips had vanished from the world.

Turning to her, I gently pulled her towards me. I cupped her face again and kissed her hard on the mouth. I savoured her mouth, desperately wanting her. It felt wonderful to feel the warmth, to hear her heart pound. Blood was pounding in my ears and my greed grew.

"I want you, Chandni," I whispered against her lips. I felt her tremble in my arms as I unravelled her lush hair that fell like soft silk on her shoulders. A fragrant, tempting cloud of silk. She was like a drug, weakening all my resolves. My hands danced over her body possessively, and her purrs of pleasure transformed into moans, making me dive headfirst into temptation. A part of me was warning me to go slow but another part was urging me to take her here, right now.

But no, not like this. I wanted to make her mine on a soft, warm bed with soft pillows and fragrant bedsheets. Not on a cold slab.

I picked her up in my arms and trudged up the stairs to her bedroom. Laying her gently on her bed, I threw open the curtains of the French windows that led to the balcony. Then I turned off the light in the room.

I sat at the foot of the bed, gazing at Chandni who now lay bathed in moonlight, lost for words. I wanted to tell her how much I loved her and express all that was raging inside me. But emotions had tied my tongue, and my blood thrummed under the surge of adrenaline. I had never seen anything as peaceful and heart-warming as this. I now knew exactly why I had impulsively carried her up here instead of the bedroom downstairs. I wanted to make love to her as moonlight bathed her in pearly white light.

I heard her sigh when I lay down beside her. Whispering endearments, I wrapped her in a crushing embrace. My mouth opened over hers in a wildly arousing kiss and heat raced through me. I stroked her shoulders, her back and my hand glided through her hair. When my fingers finally landed on the zipper of her dress, she froze.

Was all this too soon for her?

Was I rushing her?

Maybe I was. Chandni had shut her eyes tight and was clutching the bedsheet as if she was scared. I had momentarily forgotten that no man had ever touched or kissed her the way I had done.

Exhaling deeply, I sat up. The moon outside shone like a beacon of peace.

"Don't be afraid, Chandni," I said, "I won't touch you against your wish. And believe me, I can wait."

Chandni's eyelids fluttered like a butterfly and she slowly opened them. The emotion in her eyes was not fear.

"I am just nervous, that is all. I have never done anything like this..." she said as she sat up.

I gazed into her eyes not knowing what to do. "Should I go?"

"No. Make me yours," she whispered. Leaning closer, she pressed her lips against mine.

With a low groan, I kissed her with fierce tenderness and shuddered with desire when she guided my hand to the zip of her dress.

She shivered as her dress fell away beneath my exploring fingers. I slid my tongue across her lips, urging them apart. Bravely, she opened her mouth and drew my tongue into her mouth, submitting fully to my intimate caresses. Encouraged, I slid my hands down to cup her breasts, kneading them. Her nipples puckered against my palm, sending shivers of delight down my spine. Liquid heat raced through me as I dipped my head and sought her breasts. I tasted her skin by drawing tiny circles with my tongue on her heated skin. My wandering lips closed over her nipple and I bit them lightly making her arch against me. I continued to suck and pleasure them as she writhed under me.

Her moans made my heart leap, her sighs made me purr with satisfaction. I had never thought that caressing someone would bring me this much pleasure. Her warm skin blossomed under my fingers and the enchantment dragged me deeper and deeper towards ecstasy. I enjoyed undressing her but I forgot what happened to my own clothes. Maybe she removed them or I threw them away in a haste. All I wanted to feel and remember was the way her naked skin felt against mine, the way our bodies danced together to a piece of music only we could hear, the way our bodies made love and our souls sang.

An eternity later, she screamed my name in pleasure and came apart in my arms. I bent my head, devoured her lips and drove into her one last time, allowing streaks of pleasure to conquer me completely.

21

CHANDNI

Love was looking at the stars together. Love was cuddling under the moonlight hearing a lark sing. Love was sharing stories and making wishes as shooting stars shot past. We were enthusiastic newbies discovering more and more ways to love.

Karan had wrapped the white duvet around us but other than that there were no barriers between us as we sat on a lounge chair on the balcony watching the now moonless sky. The moon had set long ago and the horizon was slowly showing streaks of colour, but we had no intention of sleeping yet. It felt such a waste of time to just sleep when we could talk to each other, laugh, kiss and make love.

I don't remember when we finally fell asleep or when we returned to the bedroom. When I woke up hours later, it was past noon. Karan was still asleep and had his arms around me. Softly and carefully, I freed myself from his embrace and plodded to the attached bathroom.

I dressed quietly and headed down after a quick shower and prepared a brunch. Karan was sitting on the bed when I re-entered the bedroom half an hour later. He scowled at me. What was with that scowl?

"I've brought food for you," I said, keeping the lunch tray on the bed.

He picked up a piece of toasted bread and bit on it. Then he scowled again. "I wanted to wake up with you in my arms," he said.

His words stirred a well of love deep within me. Even his scowls were sweet. He fed me a piece and then picked up the tray and kept it on the bedside stand. Then he dragged me back to the bed and punished me thoroughly for my errant behaviour.

The next two days passed by with a mixture of lovemaking and roaming around the beautiful locales in and around Keukenhof.

On Sunday, we returned to Amsterdam. Karan's mom appeared thrilled to see us. She had tons of things to show and discuss with us regarding the wedding. Karan sneaked into my room that night right after his mother left the room after showing me the various preparations she had done for the wedding.

"I won't be with you the whole day tomorrow. Will that be okay?" Karan asked, just as I closed the door after him.

"Mom has plans to go shopping with me. After discussing with our wedding planner, she has plans for doing some shopping here. So, we will be busy the whole day tomorrow."

"Mom gets carried away when she goes shopping. Keep an eye on her. Or we will pay the price on the wedding day."

Cocooned in his arms, as I slept that night, my heart blissful and body well-loved, suddenly an unknown fear accosted me. I felt as if this was just a dream from which I would suddenly wake up. I would find myself back in the Malhotra Mansion working like a common maid and attracting only bad luck.

I couldn't understand why I was feeling the way I felt. Maybe it was because a joyful phase had never lasted this long in my life. I had never been valued, loved and cherished as I was now. Happiness was always fleeting. I snuggled closer to him as the anxiety refused to leave me. As if he had sensed my fear, Karan pulled me closer and buried his face in my hair. His warmth enveloped me, and the pace of my heart began to slow down. All was well again.

The next day, I missed him dearly every second he was away. Karan's mom took me to the many shops on her list and by mid-afternoon, I was tired to the bones. Maybe it was because Karan was away, the same fear from the previous night returned. I suddenly felt queasy as we were shopping for lace-edged table runners at a shopping mall that was famous for handmade items. The salesperson was taking down rolls and rolls of laces and Karan's mom wanted to see everything they had got. I got bored after a while and asked if I could go out and get some fresh air. The small park nearby seemed like a perfect place to get refreshed.

I found an empty bench near a fountain in the park and opened the book I was carrying. After reading for a few minutes, I felt thirsty. I had seen a coffee shop near the park gate. Karan's mom would also probably love a latte.

When I entered the cafe, I suddenly understood why I hadn't been able to shake off the feeling that something unexpected was going to happen since last night. Right there, sitting and sipping from her cup of coffee was Neeru Aunty. Seeing me, her face lit up. Somehow, her smile spiked my fear. Grandma often used to say that Neeru Aunty was like an evil creature who would intentionally trick us to take the wrong path.

"What a pleasant surprise! I heard you are going to marry Karan Varma. I always knew you would marry someone fine. You've got the looks after all. I am so happy for you," she said, as she walked toward me and invited me to sit at her table.

"Are you alone?" I asked though I knew Neeru Aunty always travelled to Amsterdam with Lavanya every year. It was from her travel photos that I had fallen in love with tulips.

"Lavanya is with me. She is at the hotel, too tired to walk around."

"Oh okay. Okay then. Karan's mom will be waiting for me. I will leave," I said and stood up to leave.

"That's not fair. Let me treat you to at least a cup of coffee. Their cupcakes are delicious. You should try some. Wait here. I will get them," she said and walked to the counter.

What had happened to her? Was she being so nice to me because I was getting married to Karan? Must be. Never in my life had Neeru Aunty bought me anything. It was a pleasant change and I decided to enjoy it for once. I watched as she brought me coffee and cupcakes.

"These are quite delicious; try them. I particularly love the ones here," said Neeru Aunty, as she stuffed one cupcake into her mouth.

I sipped my coffee and picked up a cupcake. When I swallowed the first piece, I felt the same anxiety again. As if I had done something that I was not supposed to do. And the strangest thing was nothing seemed off. The cupcake tasted delicious. The coffee too was great.

Once I finished the cupcake, Neeru Aunty said she needed to go and rushed off. I went to order a latte for Karan's mom and asked the waiter about the flavour of the cupcakes that I had eaten. I wanted to buy a few for Karan and his mom.

"We have run out of stock, ma'am. We make only a few of them every day as many people these days are allergic to peanut butter," said the waiter and fear gripped me. I had a severe peanut allergy.

At every restaurant we visited, we had specially asked for peanut-free dishes. Once in my childhood, I had nearly died after eating a savoury snack that had peanuts in it. Neeru Aunty knew about it.

Fear has the capability to intensify our disease symptoms. The most practical thing to do then would have been to ask the waiter for help immediately, but I couldn't even utter a word as nausea gripped me and I ran to the restroom. As soon as I entered the toilet, I threw up whatever I had eaten into the commode. As I retched repeatedly, I began to feel breathless. The peanuts were beginning to show their might. I couldn't even get up from the floor of the toilet. Frantically, I dialled Karan's Mom. She didn't pick up. She probably didn't even hear it ring. She kept her phone usually in silent mode all the time while travelling. Next, I dialled Karan. He didn't answer as well. His phone was perhaps in silent mode.

I called for help but as it was mid-afternoon, the cafe was almost empty and so was the restroom. Nobody came in.

I banged on the toilet door calling for help. I tried calling Karan again. As luck would have it, the phone slipped from my weak hands and fell into the commode. I couldn't even bring myself to pick it up. Just then, when I was nearly out of breath, I heard voices.

"Is someone in there?" shouted someone from the outside.

"Yes, help me please," I said dragging myself up to stand.

The next moment the door sprang open. It was the waiter. He had another male customer with him. I was having difficulty to even explaining what had just happened.

"Peanut allergy... Please help..." I managed, before passing out on the cold floor.

22

KARAN

I picked up my phone after the first series of meetings ended. Two missed calls from Chandni. That was very unusual of her. She knew I was in a meeting and would have never called unless it was an emergency. When I called her back, it wouldn't connect. The message from the service provider said the phone was switched off. Had the phone battery died? The last call was from an hour ago. She hadn't called after that. Had Mom fallen sick? She had seemed perfectly alright when I had left in the morning.

Next, I dialled Mom's number. Her number was engaged. I tried calling her again after a few minutes but it remained engaged. Using the tracker app on my phone I checked Mom's location. It showed that she was inside a shopping mall. I heaved a sigh of relief. Perhaps she'd made Chandni call me to check about some trivial detail as they shopped.

I was about to get into the meeting room again when my phone rang. It was Mom.

"Karan, do you know where Chandni is?"

"No... I thought she was with you," I said as panic gripped me.

"She left more than an hour ago saying she wanted to take a stroll in the nearby garden. I am getting worried now. Her phone is also switched off. I have been trying her phone continuously for the past half an hour."

"Don't panic. Be right where you are. I will be there in minutes," I said as I entered the elevator. Luckily, the mall where she was in was at a distance of just fifteen minutes from the workspace we had hired for the meetings. I found her in the lobby of the mall, all flustered and tired. I hired a taxi and sent her off to the hotel.

The area near the mall was full of shops. The first thing I did was to contact the local police. I provided them with all the details and then went out looking for Chandni myself. The park had only a few people and I asked around. showing her picture, if they had seen her. No one had seen her. There was a coffee shop next to the park. Could she have gone in there?

When I entered the cafe, the waiter greeted me. When I showed Chandni's picture, he recognized her immediately.

"Yes, that is her. She accidentally ate a cupcake that had peanuts," he said.

"What? Where is she now?" I asked, grabbing the waiter by his shirt.

"Sir, no need to panic. She is okay and at the hospital now. A customer took her there."

I wanted to beat the man to a pulp. How could he serve peanuts without telling her of its presence? She wouldn't have bought it if she knew.

"She would never have bought it if she knew it contained peanuts. I will sue you for not disclosing the ingredients."

"Sir, but she didn't buy it. The older lady who was with her bought it for her."

"Older lady? Who?"

"I don't know. I thought they were family. They were talking to each other and shared the cupcakes."

Who was it? For the life of me, I couldn't deduce who it could be. Deciding to leave the matter for a later time, I headed to the hospital where Chandni was.

It was just a block away and I breathed in relief when I saw Chandni lying on a bed in the emergency area. A nurse was with her, adjusting the flow of the solution from the IV bag.

I ran to her. "How is she? Is she okay?"

"Yes. She is. She is dehydrated but out of danger."

I wiped my face taking in Chandni's frail form. I couldn't understand what made her eat those cupcakes. She was always careful. I called Mom and let her know about Chandni. She was alarmed but agreed to stay at the hotel on my insistence. I stayed at Chandni's side waiting for her to wake up. The last few hours when I couldn't get a hold of her had felt like a lifetime.

I felt empty inside. I had ignored the calls from my manager continuously. Now that I had found Chandni, I should let him know. When he heard the news, he said he would talk to the clients. He called me back after a few minutes saying he had rescheduled the meetings for later in the evening. I would have liked it if the meetings were rescheduled to the next day, though I knew it was impossible. Some of the clients attending a joint meeting would be leaving Amsterdam tomorrow morning.

I wasn't ready to leave Chandni's side until she woke up. I had to see for myself that she was alright if I had to sit through hours and hours of business meetings. I sat beside her, allowing her to sleep off her fatigue and recover completely.

The emergency ward was a hub of activity with new patients arriving at frequent intervals. The on-duty nurses and doctors at the tiny hospital looked exhausted as they attended to their many patients. Most of the patients who were admitted were elderly locals though some were foreigners.

Finally, after an hour or so, Chandni woke up. I hugged her tight when she lay there looking frail yet happy. We left the hospital after the on-duty doctor checked her vitals once again.

By the time we reached the hotel, I had already received multiple calls from my manager as the joint meeting was to begin in an hour. I had so many documents to review before the meeting started. I had to rush. Thankfully, the clients had been understanding enough when my manager had told them that I was dealing with a family emergency. But now I needed to get back. Leaving Chandni in Mom's care, I left the hotel for the business centre.

Never had I wanted to rush through the meetings the way I did that day because nothing seemed as important as being back near Chandni. But never had meetings dragged on, with clients demanding my attention like never before.

All I could do was take breaks in between to call and talk to Chandni. And every time I did that Chandni reassured me to stop getting worried and finish my meetings.

23

CHANDNI

As the warm water from the shower swirled down and washed away the grime from the day, I wished it could take away the bad memories from the day as well. But they seemed to have become imprinted in my brain. Every moment of panic, pain and desperation played like a loop in my mind's eye. And the same doubt kept popping up again and again.

Had Neeru Aunty bought me those cupcakes realizing what they could do to me?

Was that why she had walked away from the restaurant in a hurry?

Did she hate me so much that she could poison me?

In those moments, when death had been so near, all I had wished for was to see Karan once again. Even if I were about to die, I wanted to die in his arms. The last few days had been so blissful that I could have died happily. Yet, when life seemed to slip away with him nowhere near, I had prayed with all my heart for a fulfilling life. I had made promises to him, to become the mother of our babies and to grow old with him as we had lain awake under the floating stars and the moon that day after I had surrendered myself to him completely.

When I came out of the bathroom, Karan's Mom was pacing in the room. She seemed worried.

"I would have broken that door down if you had taken a few more minutes to come out. You had me so worried. You look so pale. Come and lie down," she said.

I glanced at the clock and realized that I had been in the bathroom for close to half an hour. Caught in the swirl of my thoughts and the comfort of the warm water, I had forgotten that she had instructed me to keep the bath time short.

"I am okay, Mom. I feel better now," I said, but she didn't look convinced.

"Ah, I remembered something. Karan told me some older lady was with you and you had coffee together. Who was she?" she asked.

I hadn't told anyone that it was Neeru Aunty who had bought me the cupcakes. How had they known?

"How did he know?"

"The waiter told him. Who was she?"

"Neeru Aunty..." I said with some hesitation.

"Neeru, that monster? Does she know you have a peanut allergy?"

"I am not sure. I had narrowly escaped death once in my teenage years after eating a sweet made of peanuts. I am not sure if she remembers it."

"Of course, she remembers it. If something of that sort happened in my household, I would never forget it. I would make sure that the individual did not come even as close as a mile to a peanut."

"I am not sure. She treated me like a servant when I lived there. And why would she want to get rid of me now that I am not even living with her?"

"You are so naive, Chandni. That lady would do such a thing just out of spite. Almost everyone in our social circle knows that she is filled with malice."

"I agree that Neeru Aunty is not a nice person. But I don't want to believe that she is evil enough to want to kill me. I mean, I haven't ever done anything to harm her. In a way, I had moved out of her home and she was not responsible for me anymore. Why would she harm me?"

"You don't know her true colours. I have heard so many rumours about her evil nature. She wouldn't want someone she considered her servant to climb higher in social strata than her, would she? When Karan marries you, she won't be able to look down upon you anymore. For some people, the very thought of someone weaker suddenly becoming more powerful than them would be enough to take desperate steps. Also, Karan was supposedly dating Lavanya, remember? They had fuelled that news like anything. So much that their sinking stock prices had started to rise with the expectation that Karan would do something to revive the dying Malhotra Group. But when he announced his engagement with you, all of that died a quick death. Now can you believe that she has enough reasons to hate you?"

I sat on the bed and exhaled. Did Neeru Aunty hate me that much? Even though I didn't like her, I didn't hate her. I had lived in their home for years and, though it had been a colourless existence, it had not been horrible. I'd never starved and had a roof over my head always, thanks to her. I had been thankful that she hadn't thrown me out after Grandmother's death even though she had been the last link in the chain that connected us.

"So, she might try to harm me again? Is that what you are saying?" I asked, voicing my fear.

"Yes. Tell Karan about this and make sure you are never in her vicinity anymore. I had thought of inviting her to the wedding as she is your only living relative. But not anymore."

"Okay. I will tell Karan."

"What will you tell me?" A voice I dearly loved sounded in the room.

"It was that devil Neeru who tried to poison her," Karan's mom said without wasting another moment.

"What? How could you trust that woman?" shouted Karan. His face had gone all red and for a minute, he stood rooted to the place. He seemed to be trying hard to control his anger. Then he picked up his phone and began to dial.

"Whom are you calling?" asked Karan's Mom, walking toward him.

"The police, of course. That lady deserves to be behind bars."

"Don't be ridiculous. She would just say she didn't know about the allergy. We don't want anything to do with her. Let this slide this time. But if she attempts to harm even a hair on my child again, I promise you, I will make sure that she pays for it," said Karan's Mom, as she pulled the phone out of Karan's hand and cancelled the call.

I stood watching the two of them argue as to whether to report Neeru Aunty. Both laid out strong arguments and I was at a loss as to whom to support.

"That is why now I am going to destroy them. I have already purchased half the shares of Malhotra Group. You are now the biggest shareholder of the Malhotra Group," said Karan addressing me. His mom was also taken aback by his declaration.

"Why? That is a dying company. Why would you take over that trash?" said Karan's Mom.

"Chandni, I think that the Malhotras somehow made your father hand over the company to them. He had given them a Power of Attorney giving full control of the company to Ratan Malhotra before he left for Bali. Going by what she did to you today, I believe they might have been behind the sudden death of your parents too. The shareholders from whom I bought the shares believed that there was something suspicious about their deaths. Your father had no reason to commit suicide at that time, according to them. The profits were high and he had no debts whatsoever as was rumoured. No investigation was done and the case quickly closed calling it a clear case of suicide."

Though I had heard Grandma voicing the same ideas, I had never thought that they were true. She had been very proud of my father, knew how hardworking and upright he was. The thought that he could commit suicide must have hence made no sense to her.

"But Karan, wouldn't I be doing the same thing as what they did to my father? My father's company, the Venus Group no longer exists. The current Malhotra Group was built on my parent's ashes if your suspicions are right. I don't think I want to own it. I would rather create something on my own," I said.

"I agree with you, Chandni. There is no need to own trash," repeated Karan's Mom. Even the idea of being associated with the Malhotra Group didn't seem palatable to her.

"Whatever you both say, I am going to take over the group and then I will sell it to someone who wants to run it. The Malhotras must be reined in," said Karan and stomped out of the room.

The discussion put Karan in such a bad mood that he didn't come back to my room until I slept. But when I woke up sometime during the night, I found him near me, his arms wrapped around me and his face buried in my hair.

I traced my fingers on his face, and when they reached his lips, he woke up and stopped their progress.

"I am sorry if what I said before gave you pain. I believe you should avenge your parents. Your parents deserve that. You deserve that," he said.

"As you say, Karan. You know better about business than me. If you think taking over the Malhotra group will help me in some way, I will do it. You are my present and future. If you think I have to pay the debts of the past to begin my new life, I will do just that. Let's give the Malhotras a taste of their own medicine."

Karan kissed me hard on my mouth then and his hand undid the ties of my night suit. And with tender caresses that drove me wild, he began to take me into a world where pleasure reigned supreme.

KARAN

"So, you are saying you don't know where Chandni is?" I asked, unable to shake off the feeling of unease.

"I didn't say that. All I am saying is that she has gone out to meet her friend Vani. Her phone battery must have died. Maybe that is why she is not answering her phone." Mom was trying her best to not let me get worried. But I knew she was worried. Else, she wouldn't have called me to check if I had heard from Chandni.

"Do you have Vani's number?" I asked, trying to act calm even as worry began to colour my thoughts.

"I have her number and called her. But her phone is switched off as well."

"Do you know where she lives? Chandni must have gone there, right? Raju must have dropped her there, right?"

"No, she went by taxi. I had sent Raju to pick some stuff for my office," said Mom.

"Didn't you ask where they were meeting?" I asked, grabbing my car keys from my table and getting out of my office. My assistant asked where I was headed and I mouthed 'urgent' as I waited to hear Mom's reply.

"Sorry. I was on the phone. She wanted to give Vani the wedding invitation herself. As Vani was in town, she said she wanted to go and meet her in the morning."

How could she have been so careless? I had clearly explained to Mom what the situation was and why it was dangerous to let Chandni go alone anywhere.

"Vani used to stay at that PG accommodation, right? Maybe they are there. Text me the location, and I will go and pick her up," I said, trying to calm myself down.

Relax, Karan, she will be there. She will be safe.

After we returned from Amsterdam, I had been raring to teach Neeru Malhotra a lesson. The best way, I had decided, was to take away the Malhotra Group from them. When money and power went, people learned lessons faster.

Every day, I had been expecting the Malhotras to retaliate, either through words or action. Nothing had happened. Somehow their inaction had been nagging me all these days. Let this not be how they were going to teach me a lesson. Let Chandni be safe.

I had seen Vani only a few times, but I recognized her when she came down the stairs of Krishna Vilas, the PG accommodation she had been staying at along with Chandni during their college days. The surprise on her face on seeing me made my hopes vanish. Chandni was not with her.

"No, I didn't message her to meet. In fact, my phone is missing since morning. I called Chandni yesterday night, but today morning I lost my phone."

"Lost your phone? Where did you go?"

"I didn't go anywhere. Some old classmates had come to meet me."

"Could any of them have taken your phone? Would any of them play a prank on Chandni by messaging her from your phone? Because Mom said you were meeting her," I asked.

"Why would they? They all have their own phones, no?" she said, but then paused a second to think. "Maybe it was Lavanya! She always loved playing pranks on Chandni. I had even wondered why she had come to visit me with my other friends. It's not as if we were good friends in college."

Again, the mention of Malhotras. I should have left them alone. I shouldn't have done anything that would have put Chandni in harm's way.

Sitting inside my car, I pondered as to what must have happened. If Vani's phone had disappeared after Lavanya had been with her, it couldn't be a coincidence. If the mother was cunning enough to stealthily feed Chandni cupcakes laced with peanuts, the daughter could use her friend's phone to lure her out from our house.

A phone call to Mom confirmed that Chandni had not returned. It was already five hours that she had been out of contact. Not a thing Chandni would do. I headed straight to the Malhotra Mansion.

The gates were closed and the security came out when I rang the bell.

"Are you here to see the house, sir?" he asked.

"See the house? No, I am here to meet Mr Malhotra."

"The Malhotras don't live here now, sir. The house has been put on the market since the beginning of this month," he said.

"Where do they live now?"

"I don't know, sir."

"Can I look around the house then?" I asked, to confirm what he was saying.

As I stepped into the house, I understood that the house was uninhabited. Most of the furniture was covered with white sheets. I called Mom again as I walked through the house swiftly, opening and closing the many doors in the four-storeyed mansion. I told her to ask among her acquaintances as to where the Malhotras lived now. When I opened and closed the last room in the mansion and found it empty, my heart sank. Where could I find them? Could Mom help me find them and through them find Chandni? If they harmed Chandni even slightly, they were going to pay heavily.

Knowing that I could not rely on Mom alone, I called my friend, a friend from college who now worked for the phone company that was the service provider for all the phones that we owned.

"So, you want me to trace the last location of Chandni's phone? Are you sure you are not up to some mischief?" asked my friend cheerfully. I could hear him clicking keys on his computer even as we spoke. Perhaps my angst was pretty evident in my voice.

After five minutes, the location of Chandni's phone arrived as an email on my phone.

"I don't think there is any need to panic. It shows a park. I think your girlfriend just lost track of time," he said gaily as he disconnected the phone.

Losing track of time? That did sound like Chandni. She preferred walking in parks for hours together and could have very likely gotten lost in a book if she found a quiet nook to read. My pragmatic mind was calming me down laying down the facts as to why Chandni would be there at the location whose coordinates I had now entered as the destination on my car GPS.

Once I arrived at a street near the location, I clicked on the coordinates and opened it using the Google Maps application on my phone. The path ahead was too narrow to allow a car to drive through.

I walked through the narrow lanes just as the map guided me.

"Your destination is on your right," said the voice from the navigation system. I looked to my right. To my right was a badly maintained park with a 'No entry. Under maintenance' sign posted on the gate. My heart sank.

I called the friend again. "Are you sure you got the correct coordinates?"

"I am sure. The phone had been stationary for more than an hour before it got switched off, according to our records," he said.

As unease wormed through me, I looked towards the park again. Near the gate, shaped like a duck with a big belly stood a recycle bin with a sign that said 'Use Me'. On a hunch, I walked towards it and peeked into the bin.

Right atop, untouched by grime and dust, lay a phone. The phone I had gifted Chandni just a week ago.

I sank to the ground. As my knees hit the ground, I raised my head heavenwards and screamed in frustration. I had to inform the police now.

My phone began ringing just then. The number was not a familiar one but as it rang, two thoughts sprang into my mind as if someone was shouting the words aloud to me.

First, Chandni had been kidnapped.

Second, I was about to hear from the kidnapper.

25

CHANDNI

Birds were chirping somewhere near. I could hear the sound of traffic, slightly muffled as though from a distance. My head throbbed as though a truck had overrun it. My eyelids failed to listen to my wish even though I tried to pry them open. It was as if I didn't have the required energy. My mouth felt dry.

I tried to move but I couldn't. I tried again and became aware of the ropes that bound me tightly to something. I tried to think, searching for answers, allowing my mind to come up with the right questions that would give me the answers.

Where was I? What had happened to me? Why am I here?

As my mind finally caught up with what had happened, I remembered how it had all started.

I need your help urgently. Please come to the location I am texting you. I hope you won't tell anyone about this. Not even to Shweta.

Vani's text had sounded urgent and disturbing. She was not the kind of girl who got into any kind of mess usually. If it was Shweta, I would have believed that. But anything could happen to anyone these days. People changed. The very people we thought we knew inside-out, might show us an unexpected colour all of a sudden. If Vani thought I couldn't involve Shweta in this, then it was something grave. Vani and Shweta had been friends even before they met me. Had something gone wrong between them? I had walked out of the house hounded by these thoughts after telling Karan's mom that I was going to meet Vani.

When I finally arrived at the park after following the Google Maps route to the location, I had been gobsmacked to find that she had asked me to meet at a place that was completely deserted. Though it had been mid-morning then, nobody was around for as far as I could see. I had waited for more than half an hour, feeling uneasy, dialling her number again and again. The suspicion that something was wrong kept me company. After waiting for a few minutes more, I had started to walk back to the main street.

It was at this point that a bike had stopped suddenly at my side. A man riding pillion dashed toward me, making me step backwards in alarm. Before I could understand what was happening, he caught me and pressed a piece of cloth to my nose. I must have passed out after offering very little struggle because I didn't remember a thing beyond that.

With the realization that I was a prisoner now, I fought against the heaviness of my eyelids and opened my eyes a little. Everything appeared blurry initially.

"Water... I want water..." I muttered, as I swallowed painfully.

Immediately, someone splashed water on me. The cold splash awakened me a bit more. I looked around. I was in my old room in the annexe of the Malhotra Mansion.

"So, you are awake. You took your time," jeered Neeru Aunty. Her husband was pacing in the background.

"Neeru, we should let her go. This is too dangerous," said Ratan Uncle.

"Will you shut up? If you weren't this incompetent, this day wouldn't have come," Neeru Aunty sneered at her husband.

What was it that they needed from me? Had they brought me here to get back their company?

"You ungrateful bitch, how could you do this to us? Sign back all the shares you own or you will be dead," she said pushing a side table towards me. On it was a stamp paper that looked like some kind of agreement.

I didn't want their company and my first urge was to comply with their wishes. That was until Neeru Aunty opened her mouth again though.

"Your parents suffered an early death because your father treated us like vermin. Once he became rich, he made Ratan his manager and treated him like a slave. All the money went to him, and my husband got none. While your mother showed off her branded clothes, I walked around, hiding in knock offs. How could they forget that we were members of the same family? I made sure they paid dearly." Neeru Aunty seethed. "Ratan wanted me to spare you and take care of you. He feared the wrath of God, you see. But I allowed you to live because I enjoyed watching you suffer. You were never to have a bright future. But then, you captivated the boy I found for my girl. Obviously, you deserve to die too."

Her every word darted at me like poison arrows. Even though she had tried to kill me in Amsterdam, I had forgiven her because she had raised me. I had even refused to believe that she was truly evil even though Karan and his mom had laid out the evidence. But was Ratan Uncle also part of her schemes?

Neeru Aunty pushed the table closer to me and tapped on it again. Then as if this wasn't scary enough, she pulled out a knife.

"How I would love to disfigure that sinful face of yours that has rescued you from poverty," she said running the edge of the knife on my face. Involuntarily, my whole body trembled.

"Let me make her sign it, Mom. After all, she is my prey. I trapped her, didn't I?" Another familiar voice. Lavanya. She strutted toward me and smiled. A smile laced with malice.

"That's my girl. Go ahead," said Neeru Aunty.

"Lavanya, stay away," snapped Ratan Uncle.

Neeru Aunty stomped toward Ratan Uncle and caught him by his arm.

"You will stay out of this," she sneered at him. "Make sure to have some fun," she told Lavanya before leaving the room, dragging Ratan Uncle along with her.

Lavanya picked up the knife Neeru Aunty had left on the table and smirked at me. Then, she let it drop to the floor noisily. The tip of the knife got bent due to the fall.

"You are such a fool, Chandni. You enjoy wandering back into her clutches, don't you?"

"What do you mean?"

"You should have just left and never come back into our lives again," she said, leaning on the window sill. She turned away and gazed at the grounds outside. Silence filled the room, making me wonder as to what she was planning. She loved to hurt me with words. Was she going to choose a more painful route this time, I thought, looking at the knife that was shining on the floor?

"Do you remember how Grandma used to tell us bedtime stories? We would use the stories as scripts for our plays. I was always the prince who came on a white horse to rescue you, the unhappy princess. You played your part perfectly; tears came to you easily," said Lavanya.

That was so long ago. Before she had turned on her bitch mode. Why was she recounting this now?

"Do you remember when I ceased being your friend and became your biggest tormentor?" she asked, turning to gaze at me. Then, as if the memory was painful, she winced and looked away.

I remembered. It was on the day of Grandma's funeral when we were in the final year of graduation. I had been crying all night the day she died. Lavanya had been nowhere around. When I went in search of her in the morning, I had found her unconscious on her bed. When she regained consciousness, the first thing she did was to push me out of her room.

"Get lost. I don't want to see your bloody face anywhere near me, do you hear?" She had screamed at me, her eyes bloodshot and face swollen. She had loved my Grandma, probably more than I did. Her death had changed everything between us. My sweet friend had suddenly turned into a bully.

"Yes," I replied. "I lost my best friend and Grandma on the same day."

"Did you ever wonder why?" she asked as she walked towards the door. Once there, she turned the key in the lock. Then with a determined air, she approached me. Strangely, the emotion on her face reminded me of my old friend. It was the same look that she wore when we were partners in crime.

She knelt on the floor and slowly began untying the ropes that bound me.

"I watched Grandma die," she whispered, her voice so low that I almost thought I had imagined it.

"What?"

Grandma had slipped on the stairs on that fateful day and had been declared dead on arrival at the hospital.

"She did not slip and fall from the stairs. My mother pushed her from the second-floor landing and I couldn't do anything to stop her," she said, her hands clutching mine.

"That day, I was sitting in the attic bedroom reading when I heard noises. Grandma was arguing with Mom as always for doing something bad to you. Their argument escalated, and Grandma began cursing my mother for usurping the company from your parents. You know how many times Grandma had accused her of that. But that day, Mother flew into a rage and shouted, admitting that not only had she taken over the company but had also killed them. That she had paid money to have them killed. Grandma slapped her and a scuffle followed. Mother was shouting saying that she was planning to send Grandma and you to them soon. I ran down to stop their fight, prepared to help Grandma. But before I reached the second-floor hall, Mother had pushed her off over the balustrades. I could only watch as our dear grandmother fell to her death." Lavanya burst into tears.

I couldn't believe what I had just heard. Lavanya had confirmed what had been just a rumour before. I had heard housemaids whispering about it. But I had thought that it was just a malicious rumour as most of the staff at the Malhotra Mansion hated Neeru aunty.

Wiping off her tears on her sleeves, Lavanya continued.

"The sound of her scream and her blood-splattered face haunted me for days. I began to take drugs as an act of revenge toward Mom. She wanted to use me to lure a rich husband to save our sinking company. I made sure people knew me as an arrogant bitch, slut and drug addict. I was angry with you as well. Because, in a way, Grandma died because she was trying to protect you. If you weren't the weakling that you were, she wouldn't have suffered that fate."

"You should have told this to me sooner. We always shared everything, didn't we? Happiness and grief? Why did you deal with this alone?" I hugged her. A part of me rejoiced. I had found my old friend again. Another part of me was crestfallen. I knew the wreck Lavanya was now. She was not even a shadow of her former self now.

"I am happy for you, Chandni. You are not alone anymore. You have Karan who loves you like anything. His mother dotes on you. I have watched you both from far. I played along with my parents because I wanted to put an end to all this. I want to make my mother and father pay for their sins," she said.

"No. No. I will sign over the shares to you. I don't want any of it," I said.

"Are you crazy? The moment you sign these papers, she will kill you. That unsigned piece of paper is the only thing that has kept you alive till now. Bear this for just a bit longer. Karan will be here soon," Lavanya said.

"Karan? But how?"

"Oh, I think I called and told him exactly where we have kept you as a prisoner, didn't I?" she said, a grin lighting up her face. I couldn't help but chuckle.

Just then, Neeru Aunty began banging on the door.

"Did you make her sign the papers? The police have entered our compound. We will have to escape before they get here," she shouted.

"You run and hide, Mom. She hasn't signed yet. But I will make her sign. Then I will come to you. Go. Now," Lavanya shouted, winking at me.

We heard her footsteps retreating but another fear surfaced.

"Will Karan be in any kind of danger? Let me go and check," I said, getting up and heading to the door. Lavanya stopped me.

"No. Don't. Karan won't have to fight any thugs in Bollywood style sadly. Mother doesn't have anyone other than Father with her. Lack of money can be a problem when it comes to hiring thugs, you see. She spent her last rupee to hire those thugs to abduct you. The only person you have to be scared of right now in this world is my mother who has scampered out of this building like mice running out of a burning house. She won't run far; I have made sure of that too."

"Chandni, are you there?" A voice called out and happiness flooded me. Karan, he was finally here.

Lavanya opened the door and I rushed into Karan's arms. Lavanya walked out of the room and shut the door behind us.

That day convinced me that fairy tales do come true. The prince had rescued the princess again and ensured a happily ever after. This time though, it was my childhood prince who had donned her superhero cape again to come to my rescue.

Epilogue

KARAN

One Year Later

When the board of directors applauded after Chandni completed the presentation for the perfume she planned to launch this summer, my chest swelled with pride. My princess was not only beautiful but smart too. She had single-handedly revamped the cosmetics branch of the Varma Group, giving it an organic avatar. She had renamed it Venus Cosmetics. Partly to honour her father and partly because it was the perfect name for her company—after all, the goddess Venus stood for all things beautiful.

Chandni had just returned from Paris after a fortnight-long crash course to learn the ropes for creating enchanting perfumes. The sample she had created in the class had already become a rage in our household. Our Board of Directors even gave her a new name: the girl with the Midas touch. The new line of perfumes she wanted to launch was approved unanimously after her skilful presentation.

"Girl, is there anything you can't do?" I asked when she finally returned to my side.

"Yes. Drive," she said and chuckled.

"Ah, maybe we should remedy that, shouldn't we?"

"After the disaster that happened last time?" she asked.

Before she left for Paris, I had volunteered to give her some driving lessons. It was an utter failure, to say the least. Chandni became terrified whenever we came to a crossing. Nonetheless, it had been a fun experience.

"You know what? I cycled to my class every day in Paris. And I realised I prefer a bicycle more than riding a car. Tia and I visited many interesting nooks and corners of Paris."

Tia was the friend she'd made at the workshop.

I had booked a car for her but she had chosen a bicycle?

"Cycling is the best way to travel if you want to experience the soul of a place. And cycling in Paris reminded me of the time we did the same during our honeymoon," she said and it brought back the memories. Of days when we had experienced the sheer joy of togetherness. When our spirits had soured and taught us new lessons in trust and love.

Chandni had a way of surprising me when I least expected it. I loved it when she displayed aspects of her that had lain latent all this while. She had changed. The person she had been when I first met her had been a timid girl who didn't believe in dreams. Now she crafted new dreams every day and chased after them like there was no tomorrow.

Her stand on the Malhotras was another thing that had surprised me. She had begged me to not punish them.

"Time has punished them enough already. Even though they sucked as guardians, they at least kept me safe. And think of Lavanya. She is the reason I escaped from their clutches." She had argued with me and Mom for hours to convince us to let them go free.

And I had let them go, with a warning. If they tried to harm Chandni in any way, I would hand over all the evidence I had against them to the police. Lavanya had given me all the photos and videos she had taken of them holding Chandni prisoner. Ratan Malhotra had asked for forgiveness. Neeru Malhotra had looked like a bee that had lost its stinger. They had gone back to their ancestral village vowing to start over. Chandni was still keeping in touch with Lavanya. They were back to being the close friends they once were. Though Chandni had offered to sign over all the shares she owned at the Malhotra Group to Lavanya,

Lavanya had refused. She didn't even want an executive post at the company. Last heard, she had joined as a teacher at a local school in their village and loved it there.

We had merged the Malhotra Group with the Varma group and all their textile factories were now running profitably. It was as if once the management changed, they got a new lease of life.

At home, Maya was back as Mom's assistant as Chandni was too busy with her own work to help with the charity work full time.

"Do whatever you find interesting, Chandni. Let your dreams take over your days and nights. We are here to support you in all ways," Mom had told Chandni once we had returned from our honeymoon. "I wouldn't dream of binding you to me as my assistant. You've lots to achieve. Your parents will be looking at you always. Make them proud."

And thus, Chandni had started to transform. Gone was the girl who hesitated before taking even a small step on her own. Her first project was to launch her *parijat*-scented face cream and lotion, which became an overnight success. She had worked with industry experts and skin specialists to make sure the cream was problem-free.

"Anything that we put on our skin should be edible. That is what Grandma used to say. After all, the skin absorbs it and it enters the bloodstream directly. That is why organic," Chandni had explained in the interview she had given during the launch of her new products.

"Hello...penny for your thoughts? Where are you lost?" Chandni's voice, tinged with laughter, brought me back to the present. The Board of Directors had all left and we were alone in the huge conference hall.

"Had zoned out for a while," I said. Dragging her toward me, I made her sit in my lap and embraced her tightly.

"What are you doing? Someone might come in..."

"Let them. They will go away when they see us like this."

"Karan..." She rolled her eyes.

"Yes, my dear. Did I tell you how proud I am of you?"

"Did you? I don't remember," she teased.

"Of course! I am immensely proud of my princess. And I have something special for her today. Now that we have some time before our next appointments, let me give it to you."

"What? Give me now," said Chandni with childlike enthusiasm.

I took out the small jewellery box and took out a chain with a heart-shaped pendant.

"Wow, it looks so lovely," said Chandni as she took it in her palm and admired it.

I picked it from her palm, swept her long hair to one side and fastened the necklace around her neck. "I won't mind if you don't wear the mangalsutra while you are travelling. But never take this off."

"Is this what I am thinking it is? Is this your new creation?" she asked immediately understanding what I had just made her wear.

Ever since the debacle in Amsterdam and the kidnapping incident in Mumbai, I had started to become paranoid whenever Chandni went out of reach for even a few hours. I had worked on this device for days together, correcting errors in the coding of the app and adding more features.

"Yes. It is a necklace with a GPS dot embedded in it. It charges through energy generated by body heat, is waterproof, has voice monitoring, a vibration alarm, a remote shutdown facility and can transmit location details up to the accuracy of one metre."

"Whoa, you are amazing," said she, "And how do you receive the details that it transmits?"

"On the app on my phone. Now, I can check your location and be at peace whenever I want," I said beaming at her.

"I am always near you these days, am I not? We even share the same office. Even though you furnished my new office months ago, I don't use it much. This will be wasted on me," she said touching the pendant and appearing a bit lost.

"I have made a similar one made for myself. You will be able to track me too."

"Really? Show me."

I took out an identical locket and gave it to her.

"This makes me happy. You've my heart and I have yours," said Chandni. "Hey, you should manufacture it on a commercial basis. There would be many who can make use of this. This would be beneficial for children, especially for kids with special needs who often wander off on their own and get lost."

"There you go! You always think a step ahead. I was considering it."

"That would be a good idea, Karan. Let's make that a reality. It would help many."

I chuckled seeing her enthusiasm and hugged her close.

"Now can I take my wife on a lunch outing?"

"Of course. I am craving to eat at our favourite restaurant. I even dreamt of the special *thali* lunch while in Paris. I missed it so much," she said with a huge smile.

"You didn't dream about me? You didn't miss me?"

"No. I didn't," she said, her eyes sparkling with mischief.

"You wound me," I said, rubbing my palm over my heart.

"How can I miss someone who came to visit me thrice during my fortnight-long stay in Paris? How can I miss someone who called me so frequently that I became a laughing stock at the course?"

I pouted. She continued to speak as she leaned toward me.

"How can I miss someone who is right here?" she asked, pressing her palm to her heart. Her eyes had misted with tears. "How did I get so lucky, Karan?"

"A Cinderella dress, a mask and a sprinkle of angel dust. That's how," I said meeting her eyes that were now brimming with unshed tears. "By the way, what happened to my jacket that you stole that day?"

She blushed.

"I used to hug it to sleep when I lost all hope of ever meeting you. You were someone I couldn't even dream of," she said shyly.

"Oh my! How I envy that jacket! It was near you when I was missing you like crazy. I love you," I said and gathered her to myself again.

"I love you too, Karan. Like crazy. Whenever I feel alone, I remember that magical night when you held me warmly for the first time," she said softly.

I leaned down and kissed her. But like always, one simple kiss was not enough. I kissed her long and hard, tasting and teasing her almost forgetting where we were. After a long minute when I lifted my mouth from hers, I was panting with desire like a horny monster. She could make me burn with desire with just a kiss from those luscious lips. I couldn't wait to be home and watch her writhe under me, as she screamed my name in ecstasy.

I had never thought I would come to care about someone this much. She was my inspiration, my daily energy shot and my thinking buddy. It was easy to shoot off ideas with her, which she would nourish with inputs of her own.

I wonder if Cinderella's prince loved her as much as I loved Chandni. My Cinderella had been one of her kind right from the beginning. She had proved that true love could work miracles. Like a warm winter breeze, she had melted my frozen heart. She had turned my ordinary days, which passed by without meaning, into extraordinary ones.

Minutes later, as we strolled out of the conference hall hand in hand, my heart was content and my mind chatter free. There were only rainbows ahead in our path. We were firmly on the road towards our happily ever after.

-THE END

<h1 style="text-align:center">Author Note</h1>

Writing Karan's and Chandni's story was fun right from the beginning. I knew how the story should begin and end right when the story had first occurred to me. Usually, I get the idea for the ending only when I finish plotting it. For this, however, I knew exactly how I wanted to end their story.

If you liked their story, do tell me about it.

You can write to me at authorpreethi@gmail.com

Please do not forget to leave reviews on Amazon and Goodreads. Reviews matter a lot to us authors.

You can find me on Instagram (@authorpreethi) and Twitter (@preethivenu)

Thank you,

Preethi Venugopala

SREEPURAM SERIES
Book 1: The Girl at the Wedding

A Sweet Romance Novella about Arranged Marriages, Family and Love.

Kishore is home on vacation after three years. To his horror, his family is determined to get him married this time. He creates the perfect plan to escape the matchmaking attempts of his family. Just when he thought he had everything under control, a girl from his past literally crashes into his life and turns his life upside down. Within a day, he is ready to sacrifice his bachelorhood entranced by the girl he meets at his friend's wedding.

One misstep and he acquire a rival. His own cousin, Abhishek.

What can he do to win back the love of his life?

Shreya can't believe that the handsome young man she is slowly falling in love with is the bully she hated in school. He has transformed in every possible way. She likes everything about him. But then something happens that prompts her to make a rash decision.

Would this one decision ruin her chances of finding true love?

Or would she have the courage to fight for love?

Book 2: Without You

Dr Arjun enters Ananya's life like a whirlwind, bringing with him the spirit of young love.

Does the path of true love ever run smooth?

Circumstances force them apart even though they were irrevocably in love. She becomes a victim of depression. When everything fails to return her to normalcy, help arrives from an unexpected source.

Will she ever find happiness again?

Will time allow her heart to heal and forget Arjun?

What indeed is true love?

What is that strange secret that locks all the circumstances together?

Travel with Ananya to the picturesque Sreepuram, face the chaos of Bengaluru, and relish the warmth of magical Dubai in this heart-warming tale of love, betrayal, friendship, and miracles.

Book 3: His Sunshine Girl

Can two damaged souls heal each other?

Shalini is dusky and has faced body shaming throughout her life because of it. She has gone through a lot in her life, including a failed marriage and divorce, and is at a crossroad when the story begins.

She arrives in Sreepuram as the live-in literary assistant to Arundhati Mukundan, an eminent author.

Dr.Vishal, Arundhati's grandson and a pediatrician, has seen love and loss at close quarters.

When they meet in Sreepuram, it is a reunion of two childhood friends who were once inseparable.

Will their friendship help them heal?

Isn't friendship turning into love the most beautiful thing on earth?

Would fate allow that to happen or would it play its devious role again?

This is a standalone sequel to the best seller 'Without You'. You can read this even if you haven't read 'Without You.'

This story picks up from where 'Without You' ended.

Look out for some of your favourite characters from 'Without You' taking on significant roles in this story.

Book 4: What the Stars Knew

Are our destinies written in the stars?

Meet two starcrossed lovers. Naveen and Arya.

One is a techie turned famed Vedic astrologer. The other is building her life back up from ashes.

Arya: Could someone shatter your heart into a million pieces with a single word?

Once, someone did that to me. I'd vowed to forget Naveen, became somebody else's forever only to realize that forevers don't exist.

I didn't realize the power of our shared memories until he returned.

And now, I can't stop myself from rushing into his arms.

I can't stop myself from falling for him all over again.

But Naveen is not the boy I once knew.

He now speaks of what the stars know, and unforeseen destinies.

All I care about is whether we have a future together.

Naveen: I won't survive if I lose Arya again.

The memory of us has hounded me for years.

I regret the moment I left her years ago.

I believed I could forget her.

But time has proven otherwise.

Her dark eyes still bewitch me, luring me into their depths.

But the stars tell me, she is not mine to cherish.

For the first time, I want to challenge them.

I want her to be mine forever.

What do the stars know?

What is written in the destiny of Naveen and Arya?

SRAVANAPURA ROYAL SERIES
Book 1: A Royal Affair

A British commoner in love with an Indian Prince

When Jane Worthington, a reporter with a London based entertainment channel, comes to India she is sure of two things.

Firstly, she would find Daniel Worthington, the lost twin of her beloved Grandfather and fulfill his last wish.

Secondly, now that she was in India, she was not going to think about Prince Vijay Dev Varman, the scion of the erstwhile royal family of Sravanapura, the man who broke her heart years ago.

Two seemingly impossible tasks.

Vijay always believed he knew everything about himself and his family. But when Jane storms back into his life, secrets tumble out one after the other disturbing the very thread of discipline that had granted his life a semblance of sanity.

Jane cannot refuse Vijay's offer of help but every moment with him is a torture because he is not the carefree youth she had once fallen in love with.

Will they succeed to find Daniel Worthington when every single trace of his existence seems to have been carefully wiped off by unseen hands?

Or will their quest reveal secrets that will make it impossible for them to even dream of a happily ever after?

A Suspense Novella about Second Chances in Love

Book 2: he Princess and the Superstar

A Princess in love with a Bollywood Superstar
Saketh Rao aka SR, India's latest Bollywood heartthrob, has bagged the role of a lifetime: to play Hari Varman, the doomed royal scion.

When he arrives at Sravanapura Palace with his director friend Rajeev Ratnam, little does he know that his life is about to change forever!

Princess Kritika is overjoyed that Saketh Rao will play the role of her ancestor. But when she comes face to face with the arrogant superstar she is determined to scuttle the project.

Fate, however, has different plans for them. The feisty couple is soon head over heels in love with each other.

As they uncover the secrets of Hari Varman's life, Saketh makes a discovery that can rip them apart and their new-found love.

Will the secrets and lies of the past deny them a future together?

Or will they overcome the obstacles to love?

Book 3: The Lost Princess

HOW FAR WOULD YOU GO TO PROTECT THE ONE YOU LOVE?

Ishaani, the newly crowned nightingale of the Indian music industry has it all: a dream career, a loving family and loyal friends. Yet, the man she has loved all her life will not warm up to her.

Rajeev, a hotshot movie director, has feelings for Ishaani. But, she is his sister's best friend and has been like another sibling to him. Yet, what can he do if he feels compelled to make her his own?

Then, Ishaani's life changes overnight. She is no longer a lowly commoner but a princess.

She has to make some tough decisions to protect the man she loves.

Her choices lead them both down a path filled with shocking revelations and devastating consequences.

Will true love prevail?

Or will the many twists of fate tear them apart?

Book 4: Love and Longing in Firefly Season

Rashi Ratnam, the newly minted design assistant of **billionaire fashion designer** Neel Mishra, is sceptical when she leaves on a field trip to Kerala with her temperamental boss.

It doesn't matter that she has been harbouring a crush on her gorgeous boss since forever.

The man intimidates her and is cold like ice.

Also, he hasn't still forgotten his ex-girlfriend.

At **Heaven's Cove**, the beautiful backwater island owned by Neel's grandparents, Rashi begins to see Neel in a new light. She also discovers his best-kept secrets.

It is the **firefly season**, and there is nothing that stops her from falling madly in love with Neel.

But **love** is not easy.

With Neel's jealous ex-girlfriend hovering around them stirring up troubles, life becomes strenuous.

Can they face the curve balls that fate throws at them?

Or will their love die a slow death?

But in the end, is the choice theirs to make?

Read this heartwarming contemporary love story of letting go and letting love in.

P.S: This book can also be read as a standalone romance. So, you can read this even if you haven't read the Sravanapura Royals series.

Remember When

A Passionate Love Story with the Chennai Floods 2015 as Backdrop

Dedicated to the volunteers who kept Chennai afloat during the floods

On the outside, Tara leads a perfect life. A home of her own, a handsome husband, a doting son and a promising career as an author.

But inside, she is a wreck. Her marriage is a sham and she hasn't succeeded in forgetting her one true love, Manu, the man she had wronged. The man she had almost married.

Manu, now the senior editor with a science portal, firmly believes that he has left Tara where she belonged: in his past. But in reality, he hasn't forgotten anything. Not the love nor the hurt.

Their past and present collide when they accidentally meet in **Chennai.** The city has come to a standstill after facing the worst **flood** in a century. While nature is unleashing its fury on humans, they must make peace with their past.

Will they have the courage to do that?

Can they fight the attraction that still burns bright?

Or will the bunch of people they are with, teach them new life lessons?

What is the secret that is burning Tara from within?

My Warmest Sorrow

♥ **What would you do when you come face to face with your past?** ♥

Social media which is often a source of entertainment can be a source of great sorrow as well. Especially **alumni**

WhatsApp groups, as not all memories are pleasant.

When Ajay, now an IAS officer, gets added to his **college** WhatsApp group, all his classmates welcome him warmly. Except for Jasmine.

Jasmine and Ajay were inseparable while in college. Their relationship had transitioned from being **best friends to lovers** over the duration of the engineering course. But then **fate** had intervened, and they became estranged.

Five years of silence have created a **wall of sorrow** between them. Their interactions in the class WhatsApp group are nothing like what they once used to be. Every moment churns out more anguish and unpleasantness.

Jasmine is still living with the repercussions of what had happened in the **past**. Ajay's indifference throws her into despair.

What had caused their **separation**?
Is **love** still hiding underneath their public facades?
What **lies** are they concealing?

Other Works By The Author

Short Stories
A Christmas in London
My Red Knight
Kid's Books
Anya and the Spring Fairy
The Teddy who ran away
Learn Malayalam Alphabets through English